Naked Tao

Robert Grant

Copyright © 2014 Robert Grant
All rights reserved.
ISBN-978-0-9906654-0-3
Library of Congress Control Number: 2014914306

Discover other titles by Robert Grant:

Nostrum Conspiracy
UnderBelly

Coming Soon!
Great Mother

PUBLISHING

NT Publishing Company
P.O. Box 43572
Louisville, KY 40253-0572
www.NTPublishingCompany.com

Please remember to leave a review of *Naked Tao*. You might also like

Naked Tao

.

What Others are Saying About *Naked Tao:*

"A very enjoyable read. Really looking forward to the sequel." A. Engle

"I witnessed the cosmic dance and laughed out loud! A provocative and assumption shattering piece of work." Christopher Gray

"A fast paced, quick, entertaining read, that is balanced with story line twists and emotional struggle." Jeremy Nicheols.

DEDICATION

This is dedicated to victims of unsafe medications.

ALSO BY ROBERT GRANT

BULK PURCHASES

We will gladly provide paperback copies of this book at a discounted price for bulk purchases. Send a request to Robert@NTPublishingCompany.com.

CHAPTER 1

Twice already the jury reported they were unable to reach a unanimous decision and both times the Judge sent them back for further deliberations. A hung jury is like a tie. Nobody is ever satisfied with a tie. Especially, a man like Wilbur Goth.

Goth is one of the richest men in the world and is accustomed to getting what he wants. He did not want a hung jury. Laying a heavy hand on my shoulder he told me that a win in a case like this could launch a young lawyer's career. What he didn't have to say is a loss would ruin me.

I needed that not guilty verdict as much as Goth did, but after five days of deliberations, the Judge was on the verge of declaring a mistrial, which could lead to a new trial. Goth didn't want the prosecutor to get a second bite at the apple. He wanted finality.

The Judge had cleared the courtroom while she considered the matter, so I returned to my office to await her decision, but with each passing minute, I grew less confident in the outcome.

Gaia, the firm's documents clerk, stuck her head in my office door and asked, "Have you heard anything yet, Mr. Li?"

I shook my head.

"Don't look so glum," she said with a broad smile. "You'll spoil that handsome face."

Her compliment didn't feel like a come-on. Gaia has a way about her. No matter what dark place my thoughts wander into, she always manages to lead me out. It's less about what she says and more about a strange light that radiates from her. It's as if I can see her spirit.

She is tall, maybe 6'2", dressed in a sky blue button down shirt and a black skirt just shy of indecent. Her long dark hair is woven into an intricate braid that falls straight down the center of her back. She tied the end of the braid with semi precious blue stones that match her blue eyes.

It's hard to be grumpy when she's around, so I flashed her my best smile. Funny thing about a smile, it always seems to work a strange alchemy on my mood and on the moods of everyone around me. It's as if a jolt of happiness runs through anyone who is lucky enough to come into contact with it.

"That's more like it," she said.

The smile was interrupted by the theme song from my favorite 1950's legal drama. I checked my mobile and saw it was a call from the Judge's secretary. The anxiety returned with a vengeance and I hesitated for just a moment.

"Go ahead, answer it," said Gaia.

I put on my game face and said, "Hello, this is Grant Li."

"Mr. Li, this is Judge Flint's secretary," said the young man on the other end of the air wave. "The Judge wants everyone back in court in thirty minutes."

"Do we have a verdict?" I asked.

I couldn't help but wince at the desperate tone in my voice.

He paused before answering, "I really can't say, Mr. Li."

"Thanks, I'm on my way," I said.

I dropped the phone in my pants pocket and slung a briefcase over a shoulder. I took a calming breath and reminded myself, good or bad, this was about to come to a head.

"Good luck, Mr. Li," said Gaia.

"Thank you," I said.

As she turned to leave, I asked, "Is he in his office?"

She nodded and scurried off to get some work done in the firm's file room.

John Biggs is a senior partner in the law firm. His legendary skill as a tenacious litigator is the reason I chose this particular firm. I wanted to mentor with one of the best, but lately our relationship had been strained, because John was upset that Wilbur Goth chose me to defend him.

More than once, he shook his head and said, "Why would he want someone barely out of law school to defend him against serious criminal charges? It makes no sense."

John has the big corner office and makes the big bucks, while my tiny office overlooks the pigeon infested HVAC unit perched on the adjoining rooftop. While Pathogen is based in Louisville, it is an international company with an army of lawyers all over the world representing them.

John is the company's local counsel and Wilbur Goth is the CEO. I didn't want to admit it, but John was right. Clients like Pathogen do not want a young associate attorney to defend them against serious felony charges.

John would want to know that the jury was back in the courtroom, so I headed down the hall to deliver the news. His secretary, Helen Gloria, usually guards the door to his office, but she was in the break room arguing with her tearful teenage daughter.

While most of the attorneys in the firm fear Helen, clearly her daughter does not. Helen has been known to send more than one young associate away from John's doors with his tail tucked between his legs. She is one of those women who look soft on the surface, but when you cross them, they cut you to shreds with a tongue as sharp as a Samurai sword.

Helen's daughter looked like a younger version of Helen. They were both medium height brunettes with big brown doe eyes. Their body types were soft and curvy. Mom was dressed in a white blouse and blue skirt. Her daughter wore a plain white t-shirt and blue jeans.

"I promise you I will be there, Laurie," said Helen.

"Mom, you never do what you say you're going to do," said Laurie. "Why should I trust you?"

Helen's shoulders slumped just enough to tell me that Laurie had hit a raw nerve and her half-hearted response confirmed she was losing ground.

"I'm doing the best I can," said Helen.

"No you're not, Mom," said Laurie. "You give everything you have to this job and to that tyrant you work for. There's nothing left for me."

"Show some respect, young lady," said Helen.

"Really, Mom?" said Laurie with a level of sarcasm only a teenage girl can muster. "How about you show me some respect for a change? Isn't that what we're really talking about here?"

Helen's sob was all the response I heard as I moved out of earshot and closer to John's office. It's amazing how much of a conversation you can catch just walking by an open door. In this instance, it was enough to make me think twice about ever having a teenage daughter of my own. Not that there is much chance of that since I'm currently separated from my wife, Cynthia.

Still, Laurie had made a valid point and I felt a rush of compassion for her. There are rumors about John and his secretary that are fueled by their behavior toward each other. Rarely does an office romance end well, and in this instance, it was clearly putting a strain on her relationship with her daughter. Besides, John is a known womanizer. They deserve better.

Helen is in her mid-thirties and a few years younger than John's oldest daughter. Twice married, he has a second family. His son is about the same age as Laurie, and the last I heard, they are both juniors at duPont Manual High School.

I must admit, it was a relief to move out of range of the mother-daughter battle because it sounded to me like it was going to get much uglier before it got any better. However, my relief was short lived, since I found John in his office arguing with a teenager of his own.

John is soft and gray. If I had to guess, he was born conservative. He was dressed in gray slacks and a blue blazer worn over a light blue shirt loaded with enough starch that it could stand on its own.

At first blush, he looks like a pushover, maybe a minor clerk, but certainly not a high-powered lawyer, which is exactly what he wants his enemies to think. John's son must take after his mother. He is tall, thin and blessed with runway model good looks. However, I could see he was tough like his father.

"Richard, I have a law practice to run and you're upset because I missed a football game," said John.

"Yeah right, Dad, it was just a football game," said Richard. "It doesn't matter that I scored the game winning touchdown, because it's all about you and your stupid clients."

"If it wasn't for clients like Pathogen, you wouldn't have the luxury of playing football instead of working after school like I did when I was your age," said John.

"I play football because you're never home," said Richard. "You don't get it, Dad. What I really need is a father. Do you know where I can find one?"

"That was unnecessary," said John.

"For once can you put me before Wilbur Goth?" asked Richard.

John cut his eyes toward me and said,

"Speaking of Wilbur Goth, do we have good news, Grant?"

I shrugged.

"The judge's office called," I said. "She wants us back in court."

"Is this the Goth trial?" asked Richard.

I nodded.

"It figures…the man I hate most in this world will most likely dodge justice and it's all on you, Grant Li," said Richard as he stormed past me.

John scowled, but let him leave without another word.

"Did you inform the client?" asked John.

I shook my head.

"Not yet," I answered.

John raised a bushy eyebrow. His disapproval of me was getting old.

"I just got the message and wanted to make sure you were the first to know," I said.

John gave me a begrudging nod and said, "I'll call him myself."

"Suit yourself," I said.

"Let me know how it goes," said John.

I had a feeling he was conflicted about the outcome. It wouldn't surprise me a bit to learn John wanted a guilty verdict against his biggest client just to see me fail.

"Will do," I said and turned to leave.

"Grant, you better not lose this," said John.

I looked him in eye and instead of telling him I could do without the added pressure, I simply said, "Roger that."

It's six blocks from our office to Federal Court. I prefer to walk, but usually drive when I'm loaded with files. Not that it's much help since there is nowhere to park close by thanks to the car bombing of a Federal building in Oklahoma City back in 1995. In this instance, a lightweight brief case hung from a shoulder and my hands were free of files, so I walked. Besides, I needed to clear my head.

Pathogen is the world's biggest pharmaceutical company. Last year they developed a drug called Gutchriem that is now routinely prescribed by physicians all over the world for acid reflux and other intestinal disorders. It didn't take long before patients using the drug started getting sick.

In an unusual move, the prosecutor, Zeke Kruthers, brought Federal fraud charges directly against the CEO, Wilber Goth, alleging the public was intentional deceived about the drug's risks. In typical Goth fashion, he went on the attack, using Pathogen's public relations machine to portray the case as a witch hunt that was less about the law and more about a young prosecutor's political ambitions.

It was still early spring, but unseasonably hot and humid in the Ohio Valley. The river is flanked on both sides by knobs that trap pollution, pollen, and heat which hang over the city like an oppressive blanket of smog that is hell bent on suffocating the residents. I thought about the health advisory issued earlier in the day by Louisville Metro Air Pollution Control District and second guessed the decision to walk.

Unfortunately, it was too late to turn back, so instead, I picked up the pace and breezed past the wig shops and other merchants struggling to eke out an existence on a dying inner city street. By the time I reached the courthouse steps, my crisp white shirt had melted into my skin.

A blast of cool air greeted me at the metal detectors located just inside the door. I dropped the brief case, car keys, cell phone, and suit jacket onto the conveyor belt and stepped through the detector. It was manned by a United States Marshall, named Mark Fritz, who served with my Uncle Jim in Afghanistan.

"Good luck, Grant," said Mark.

"Thanks Mark," I said as I collected my things. "It's been a tough trial."

"Aren't they all?" he said.

"No kidding," I said. "It's our way of settling disputes in a civilized society without resorting to bloodshed, but if you ask me, they are no less savage."

"I don't know about that, Grant," said Mark.

"I've seen savagery and it can scar a man for life."

Mark was right, comparing our justice system to war is foolish. I nodded and headed down the hall.

While State Court is always filled with a mass of broken humanity, the Federal Court Building feels like a mausoleum. The old marble floors are polished to a sheen, but the brass doors that once led to the post office, social security administration, and other federal offices are closed and locked. Foot traffic is limited to the few individuals on official court business, and at the moment, it was my solitary footsteps echoing along the corridor leading to the elevators.

As I exited the elevator, I checked the time and was pleased to see I had eight minutes to spare. If I was lucky, I would get a chance to sit in an empty courtroom for a few minutes before everyone arrives. It's a small pleasure that also gives me a chance to focus my thoughts on the task at hand.

This particular courtroom has a special feel to. It is old school, spacious and full of rich woodwork that I find comforting. Maybe it's because of the natural materials. I love the woods, and while I don't condone cutting down trees to fulfill man's vanity, the polished wood makes me feel like I belong there.

The double doors leading into the courtroom are at least ten feet tall and made of polished oak with brass inlays. The brass is etched with the scales of justice on one door and a blindfolded lady liberty on the other. They are perfectly balanced on their hinges and easily swing outward.

As hoped, the room was empty so I made my way to the bar, eased through the swinging gate and took a seat at the defense table. This is the only time I can relax in court and I needed it to mentally prepare myself for what was about to happen.

Taking a lesson from martial arts, I've learned that what happens in the mind shapes the events of our lives. I took a deep breath, relaxed and envisioned the foreman reading a not guilty verdict.

It was working pretty good until the curse of modern life disturbed the peaceful moment. Where ever we go, our cell phones follow us like a little puppy demanding our constant attention, but not nearly as cute.

I wanted to ignore it, but you never know when it's going to be an important call and this wasn't just any ringtone, it was Mom's long term care nurse, so I took the call.

"Is everything okay, Roxanne," I said.

"Hi Grant, it's Roxanne," she said.

"How's Mom?" I asked.

"There's an emergency, you need to get here right away," said Roxanne.

"What's happened?" I asked.

The call dropped. I tried to reconnect with her, but she didn't pick up.

CHAPTER 2

I owe Mom's nursing home a lot of money and their collection efforts have been getting more aggressive. Lately, I've been busy with the trial and ignored their calls, but they've never been cold enough to fake a medical emergency to reach me.

Mom's life could be in danger. If it really is a medical emergency, I will never forgive myself if I'm not there. On the other hand, I need to be here for the verdict. Torn in two directions, I sat frozen in my seat, struggling with an impossible situation.

I don't know how much time passed before the doors swung open and the prosecutor, Zeke Kruthers walked into the courtroom. Zeke can't be more than 5'6" and is shaped like a teddy bear. He is pushing forty and balding at the crown. What Zeke lacks in physical strength is made up with a force of will that leaves you thinking he is 6'4" and packed with muscle.

Zeke nodded respectfully in my direction and then took a seat at the prosecutor's table. I hadn't noticed before, but there was an envelope at his seat. He picked it up and turned it over in his hands, before setting it down again just as Goth entered the courtroom.

Goth is medium height and round. Not fat exactly, just round. Most people's heads are more oval than round, but not Goth's. His head is round and a size too big for the rest of him. Everything else is curved. His hips and thighs are soft and rounded, like a woman's, but that's as far as the softness goes.

Goth is edgy and dark of spirit with a head of orange hair that contrasts sharply with the black suits he always wears. I suspect there may have been a fool or two in his past who tried to call him Pumpkin Head and lived to regret it. I know that is the nickname that comes to mind when I think of him.

He extended an ice cold hand that I took for a brief moment and then quickly released.

"Let's get this over with," said Goth. "I have a meeting tomorrow morning in London."

"You seem confident of the outcome," I said.

"I'm the master of my fate," he said.

"Right now the jury seems to be struggling with your fate and the Judge is on the verge of calling this a mistrial," I said.

"You won't escape justice with a mistrial," said Zeke. "If necessary, we will retry this case."

Goth glared at the prosecutor.

"There won't be a mistrial," said Goth.

I didn't know whether he was blustering or if he knew something that I didn't know. He certainly had the resources to tamper with the outcome of a trial, but that is unthinkable and I pushed it out my mind.

Zeke turned away from Goth's glare and picked up the envelope, but then set it aside when the bailiff entered from a side door near the bench.

"All rise," said the bailiff.

Judge Sarah Flint entered the courtroom and took a seat at the bench. Federal Judges are appointed for life and Judge Flint wears the deep lines cut into her face as a living testament to a long career on the bench. She has a reputation as a brilliant jurist who is both fair and tough. Judge Flint has little patience for fools and liars.

She took a long hard look at Goth and said, "Gentlemen, the jury foreman reports we have verdict. Let's bring in the jury."

A side door opened and the jury filed into the courtroom. I studied them carefully for any sign of their decision. One juror in particular caught my attention. She was a twenty-something mother who spent a lot of time during the trial shaking her head and glaring at Goth, except now, she was smiling in his direction. I hoped this sudden switch in body language meant we had a favorable verdict.

Once the jury was seated, the Judge asked, "Mr. Foreman, has the jury reached a decision?"

The Foreman stood and answered, "Yes, your honor."

"Bailiff will you bring the verdict to the bench?" said the Judge.

The bailiff accepted a folded piece of paper from the Foreman and handed it to the Judge. She read it and then cast a hard look at Goth, before handing it back to the bailiff, who then returned it to the Foreman.

"Please read the verdict, Mr. Foreman," said Judge Flint in a hard tone.

The Foreman looked at Goth and then at the Judge. He swallowed hard, took a deep breath and then read.

"We the jury, find the Defendant, Wilbur Goth, not guilty of all charges," said the Foreman.

"Ladies and Gentlemen, thank you for your honorable service in this matter," said the Judge. "Our freedom as a nation is dependent on the honest faithful service of men and women who sacrifice their time and families to dispense justice."

It sounded like a lecture to me, rather than a heartfelt expression of gratitude and the looks on the faces of many of the jurors told me they felt the same way.

"Mr. Goth, you have been found not guilty by a jury of your peers and are free to go," said Judge Flint.

She slammed the gavel hard and brusquely left the courtroom. Not once during the trial had she used the gavel, but I wasn't about to let her antics spoil this for me.

I raised a victory fist and said, "Yes!"

I have to admit, this was one of those shining moments that we get to experience from time to time. In these rare moments, all is right with the world. Everything is perfect and possible. I was on top of the world and it felt damn good.

Goth patted me on the back and said, "Thank you for a job well done, Grant."

I shook his hand and said, "Congratulations!"

"I should be congratulating you," said Goth.

"Thank you," I said.

There was something odd in his eyes that I couldn't quite put a finger on. It was almost predatory, but then it quickly disappeared.

"You deserve everything that will come from this," he said.

Before I could say anything else, Zeke Kruthers stormed out of the courtroom. Goth watched him leave with a look of complete contempt on his face. When the door shut behind Zeke, Goth turned his attention back to me and I thought I saw remnants of that contempt in his eyes, but then he smiled and left without another word. I remembered Mom and the nursing home, so I didn't waste any time gathering my things and following Goth out the door.

When I was eight years old, all Dad ever talked about was buying a new Harley, but couldn't bring himself to do it. Instead, he would shake his head and tell Mom he had a family to think about. She had ideas of her own. Mom scrimped and saved for it anyway and on his thirtieth birthday she fulfilled Dad's dream.

Mom woke me early that morning and whispered that it was a special day. She led me down the hall to the bedroom where Dad was snoring softly. Together we pounced on him while singing happy birthday. Dad growled at us for waking him, but his eyes were shining and filled with love.

After our early morning celebration, Mom told him she was having car trouble and asked if he would take me to school. We followed him to the garage and watched as he lifted the overhead door. Instead of his car, a new Harley was sitting in his parking space. I've never seen Dad so surprised as he was in that moment.

After dropping me off at school my parents decided to take the Harley out for a maiden ride.

I never saw Dad again thanks to a hit-and-run driver. Mom…well, she lay in a crumbled heap at the bottom of a ditch for several hours before a passerby discovered her. They waited an hour for an ambulance that never showed.

The Good-Samaritan finally gave up and carried her to his car, put her broken body in the back seat and drove her to the hospital himself. Nobody knows for sure whether his good deed or the wreck caused her paralysis from the neck down, but she's been that way ever since.

With Dad gone and Mom unable to care for a child, Uncle Jim raised me, but he almost didn't get the chance. Some know-it-all social worker wanted to place me in foster care. She kept telling the Judge I needed the positive influence of a woman in my life. The social worker didn't like the fact that Uncle Jim had lived all over the world, mostly on military bases, and she was suspicious that he had never married. She was convinced that a single man knew nothing about raising a son.

That social worker picked the wrong man to attack, because Uncle Jim knows a few things about winning a fight. The Marine Corps trained him for some hush-hush special ops unit that he never talks about. A legal battle is no different than any other fight and Uncle Jim put up a tough fight. He convinced the Judge that it was in my best interests to be with him. As far as I'm concerned, the Judge made the right decision. What kind of crazy person would think foster care is better than a loving family member?

Taking care of Mom has been tough. When the insurance ran out, the doctors lost interest. I was glad because I hated the hospital. Uncle Jim brought Mom home and set her up in her old bedroom. Every day after school, I sat by her side and prayed until bedtime. I was taught that God always answers our prayers, and with the faith of a child, I prayed for God to heal her.

Days turned into weeks, then months. When I lost interest in everything else, including Chi'ng's martial arts classes, Uncle Jim decided it was time for an intervention, so he sat me down and we had a long talk.

"Grant, I know you've been praying a lot for your mother," he said.

"Yes, sir," I said with a small nod of the head.

He patted me on the shoulder and said, "She's in my prayers as well."

"Why hasn't God answered our prayers?" I asked.

"It's a funny thing about prayers," said Uncle Jim. "They are always heard and answered. It's up to us to be patient and to keep our eyes and ears open."

"I asked God to make her like she used to be,"

I said.

"Do you believe she will be?" he asked.

"Yes, sir," I answered.

"Then God has heard your prayers and he will take the appropriate action in his own time," said Uncle Jim.

"I don't want to wait," I said.

He squeezed my shoulder as he said, "I know, Grant. There's something else you should know about faith."

"What's that, sir?" I asked.

"An important part of faith is having the courage to trust that things will work out for the best in end," he answered.

"Yes, sir," I said. "Will it be okay if I keep praying?"

"Yes, it will be okay," said Uncle Jim. "In the meantime, it's our job to take care of ourselves and leave it to God to work out the details. Do you understand what I'm saying, Grant?"

"I'm not sure," I answered.

"Taking care of your mother seemed like the right thing to do at first, but now I see it's a job best left to a nurse," said Uncle Jim.

"I can do it," I said.

"I know you can, but it takes a lot of time and it's a job for a grown-up...a professional," he said.

I tried my best to keep the sadness locked

inside, but it would have none of it.

"I ca...ca...can...dddd...do it," I sobbed.

I can count the number of hugs Uncle Jim has given me on one hand. This was hands down his best effort.

When he finally pulled himself together again, he said, "I know son, but it's time to give you your childhood back. You should be playing with your friends and doing fun stuff, like martial arts with Chi'ng."

A few days later we drove Mom to Shady Days. In the years that followed a day never went by without me saying a prayer for her and hoping it would be the day she made a full recovery. That was twenty years ago.

CHAPTER 3

Shady Days is located in a historic sanatorium that was built in 1912 following an outbreak of the white plague. Uncle Jim chose it because he thought Mom would like the hilltop view of the Ohio River. Other than a central tower constructed of white stone that is now stained by years of smog, the four-story building is covered with red brick and ivy. One of the unusual features of the building's architecture is the way it curves to follow the ridgeline.

When antibiotic treatments proved effective for tuberculosis, the sanatorium was closed. After sitting empty for years, like a forgotten ghost haunting the hillside, the owners of Shady Days bought the property and converted it to an adult long-term care facility.

While the outside of the building looks antique, they spared no expense giving the inside a polished new look. The living quarters are designed like luxury apartments, complete with a comfortable living room and eat-in kitchen where residents can make themselves a snack at any hour. Since Mom is bedridden, the living room and kitchen are used by her only visitors, me and Uncle Jim.

All that fanciness makes it expensive keeping Mom there. I haven't opened a bill lately, but the last time I checked, I owe Shady Days nearly $200,000.00. I don't have the money and don't know where I'll get it. Between my wife's extravagant spending and the high costs of getting Mom the care she needs, I'm on the verge of bankruptcy.

A few months back, I worked out a payment plan with their administrative director, Alexi Minted, but after John cut my monthly bonuses I missed a few payments. When I confronted him about it, he claimed the firm's profits were down and he had to reduce attorney bonuses.

We both know that's a bunch of bull. John got a young woman in trouble and had to pay her off. Instead of using his own money to pay for his sins, he used mine.

Some of Mom's functioning comes and goes, so she has both good days and bad. The worst are the days she stops breathing and they have to put her on a respirator to keep her alive. Those are the days I fear the most. Since Roxanne didn't take my return call, I had no way of knowing whether this was one of those days or if the nursing home had stooped to an all-time low to get their money.

Fortunately, the facility isn't far from my downtown office and I expected to have an answer soon. I took River Road, a scenic byway that provides spectacular views of the Ohio River. On most days you can catch a glimpse of Louisville's small sailing community out on the water. The sailboats share the river with an authentic steam power paddle wheel and barges running coal up and down the river. The paddle wheel gives the river a whimsical, out-of-time, Mark Twain mystique.

These days my only transportation is an old pickup truck Dad left me. I kept it for sentimental reasons, but even though it is fighting a losing a battle with rust and rips off an occasional noisy backfire, I have grown fond of it.

As much as Louisville wants to be a big city, it is really a small town with loads of southern friendliness. Most folks are pleased to see you and Ginger is no exception. She mans the front desk at Shady Days and we've been on a first name basis for years.

Ginger is fifty, plump, and warm. She loves talking to people and when the administration tried to give her a promotion with more money and responsibility, but less contact with people, she rebelled.

She was wearing a classic white nurses outfit,

complete with the little white hat. If it wasn't so conservative, I would have thought she found it at a costume store. All of that white contrasted with her auburn hair and pink skin tone.

Ginger is a sweet person, but scatterbrained. Sometimes it's hard to get her to focus.

"Oh, I'm glad you're finally here, Grant," said Ginger.

"What's the emergency?" I asked.

Ginger looked around and then whispered, "It's not right."

"What's not right?" I asked.

Her eyes darted in two different directions at once as she whispered loud enough to be heard halfway down the hall, "Shhh…keep it down, would you?"

I lowered my voice, "What do you mean…it's not right?"

"I can't say," she said.

This was going nowhere, so I asked instead, "Where is she?"

"Intensive care," she answered.

I've never had a panic attack that I know of, but this had to be one. It felt like three hundred pound guerilla was jumping up and down on my chest. I tried to grab my heart, but all I got was a hand full of shirt.

"Are you okay, Grant," said Ginger. "You don't look so good."

Mom has been there before and even though she's a survivor, it doesn't get any easier. Each time, I fear this might be the one she can't win. Remembering my martial arts training, I replaced the picture in my mind of Mom dying alone in a hospital bed with an image of her sitting up in bed, brushing her hair. It was the picture of her perfect health. It helped.

Sometimes we get off track, but all it takes is a moment or two to set ourselves in the right direction, with the right frame of mind. When my hands finally stopped shaking, I thanked Ginger and headed to intensive care.

As I turned toward the elevators, Ginger said one last time, "It aint' right. There's nothing right about it."

The medical wing of the facility looks and feels just like a hospital. I'm not sure I like that since hospitals trigger such painful memories for me. On the other hand, it is reassuring to know they are equipped to respond to Mom's medical needs.

The intensive care unit is small, but seems to have all the latest medical gadgets. I found Mom surrounded by a doctor and two nurses working to resuscitate her. The panic attack returned, but this time the room felt oppressively hot. I removed my suit jacket and looked for a place to sit so I could return to the still pool meditation to calm my mind.

Mom was lying on her back. Roxanne tilted Mom's head back slightly and lifted her chin. The doctor stacked his hands, one on top of the other, in the middle of her chest. Using his body weight, he pushed hard and fast. After about a minute, he paused while the second nurse pinched Mom's nose and did several rescue breaths before dropping her ear to Mom's mouth.

The nurse looked up at the doctor and said, "She's breathing."

"We're not out of the woods yet," said the doctor. "I want to know what caused this. Put her on saline and draw some blood."

The nurses scrambled in two different directions to comply with his orders. The doctor was in his early thirties, medium height, sandy blond hair, green eyes, and physically fit. He wore thick glasses, blue jeans, sneakers and a lab coat with a pocket protector filled with ink pens and a penlight. He was both handsome and a total nerd at the same time. His nametag identified him as Dr. Michaels.

"Who are you?" he asked.

"I'm her son, Grant Li," I answered as I extended my hand. "What is wrong with my mother?"

He took my hand in a firm grip and answered,

"We don't know yet. You shouldn't be here."

"I'll stay out the way, but I'm not leaving her side," I said.

"Suit yourself," he said.

"What happened?" I asked.

"The nurse was feeding her and she started choking," he answered.

"What did she feed her?" I asked.

"One of her favorites, apple sauce," he answered.

"You wouldn't think she would choke on apple sauce," I said.

"I agree," he said.

"Anything else?" I asked.

"Sweet green tea," he answered.

"What happened then?" I asked.

"While the nurse was checking for obstructions, your mother broke into a cold sweat," said Dr. Michaels.

I felt a chill because I had heard this before.

"Was that followed by shaking?" I asked.

Dr. Michaels' eyes widened.

"How did you know that?" he asked.

"When the shaking stopped, so did her breathing," I said.

He nodded.

"How could you possible know this?" he asked.

My hands were shaking when I asked, "Is she

taking Gutchriem?"

"Yes," he answered.

"When was her last dose?" I asked.

He checked the chart and then gave me a long appraising look before answering.

"It was fifteen minutes before she was fed," he answered.

"We need to get that drug out of her system," I said.

"It is a harmless heartburn treatment," said Dr. Michaels. "It could not have possible caused this."

"Listen to me very carefully, doctor," I said. "I just spent two weeks in trial listening to evidence that Gutchriem causes those very symptoms."

Dr. Michaels slid his glasses down an inch and studied me over the top of them.

"What exactly do you do for a living?" he asked.

"I'm an attorney," I answered.

He let out a barely audible groan.

"These symptoms are not listed as possible side effects of Gutchriem," he said.

"No they're not, but there have been twelve deaths since this drug was approved by the FDA," I said. "I do not want my mother to be number thirteen."

"Thirteen," he repeated.

"Can you pump her stomach?" I asked.

He nodded.

"I need to call the poison control center first," he said.

Roxanne walked into the room and said, "Do you want me to make the call, Doctor?"

I raised my voice, "Do it now, Dr. Michaels! There is no known antidote and time is of the essence. We have to get that drug out of her stomach before any more of it enters her blood stream. Her life depends upon it."

Dr. Michaels nodded and turned to answer Roxanne, "Never mind, let's pump her now. Have you ever done a gastric lavage, nurse?"

She shook her head.

"Let's begin with an intubation," said Dr. Michaels.

Roxanne nodded before grabbing a silver device shaped like a water pistol. She tilted Mom's head back, inserted the device in her mouth and then worked a plastic tube into her throat.

I must have looked a bit pale, because she said, "This protects her trachea."

"Would you rather wait outside?" asked Dr. Michaels.

I shook my head.

"I want her in left lateral decubitus position," said the doctor.

Roxanne tilted Mom to the left and stuffed a pillow under her right side. Then she titled her head slight to the left.

"Give her a bite block in case she wakes up," said Dr. Michaels.

Roxanne added something that looks like an infant's pacifier to Mom's mouth. Dr. Michaels took blue tubing and measured from the bite block to her stomach before marking the spot with a sharpie. While he was bent over her, he placed an ear close to her mouth and listened.

He nodded in satisfaction and then began feeding the tubing through an opening in the bite block, before connecting it to a port in the hand pump that Roxanne had set near Mom's head. A second port in the pump was connected to a plastic bag on the floor.

Dr. Michaels pulled the handle of the pump back and then released it a couple of times to confirm the flow of stomach content to the bag on floor. He added some charcoal to the pump and connected a bag of water hanging from an I.V. Stand. He double checked his connections and then began pumping until nothing else came out of Mom's stomach. Roxanne removed the tubing and the pillow.

I was surprised at their speed and efficiency. The entire procedure only took a couple of minutes from start to finish.

Afterwards Dr. Michaels pulled me aside and said, "I will continue to monitor your mother's condition."

"Thanks, I'd like to see her as soon as wakes up," I said.

"We can do that," he said.

"Thank you for listening to me," I said.

"I hope you're right about this," said Dr. Michaels.

"Do you plan to run more tests?" I asked.

"Yes, I want to be sure we didn't miss anything," he answered.

"Will you let me know as soon as you have the results?" I asked.

"Yes, of course," he answered. "By the way, is your trial over?"

The trial was the last thing I wanted to talk about. I was emotionally drained and physically exhausted, but tried not to let it show to much as I nodded.

"What was the outcome?" he asked.

"We got a favorable verdict," I answered.

"Good, that will be one less dangerous drug we have to worry about," said Dr. Michaels.

Then it hit me. Gutchriem nearly killed Mom and today's verdict insures that it will remain on the market.

I excused myself, but Roxanne stopped me in the hall. She's my age, 5'6", curly brown hair, and green eyes. She was wearing blue scrubs with a wet spot on her chest from the sweat she worked up during Mom's emergency. I've known Roxanne since high school and she didn't look happy.

"I'm really sorry about everything, Grant," said Roxanne.

"No need to apologize for saving Mom's life," I said.

"It's all in a day's work and you're welcome," said Roxanne.

"I don't know what would have happened if you hadn't called me," I said.

"Yeah, it's fortunate you know so much about Gutchriem," she said. "Did you talk to Alexi?"

"The director?" I asked.

"Yes," she answered.

"No, I haven't," I said. "Does she want to speak with me?"

"Yes, that's why I called earlier," said Roxanne. "You should talk to her right away. It's important. Oh, and Grant, did I tell you I'm really sorry."

I found Alexi sitting at her desk. Even though she can't be more than thirty-eight, her retro afro looked like it was styled in the late sixties. Other than the hair, she was all 21st century style with a sharp grey business suit, white blouse, and designer glasses.

"Come in and sit down," said Alexi. "I have something to tell you."

"Look I know I owe you a lot of money, but I'll figure something out," I said.

"The Board of Directors has made a decision," she said.

"I don't understand," I said. "A decision about what?"

"Ms. Li can't stay here any longer," said Alexi.

"You can't just put her on the street," I said. "It could kill her."

"Your account will be turned over to our attorneys for collection," she said.

"Please, just give me a little more time," I begged.

"I'm sorry, Grant, but it's too late for that," she said.

I wanted to be angry with Alexi, but she looked like she had the weight of the world on her shoulders. I ran a hand through my hair and tried to think of some way to stop this, but came up with nothing. I needed time to figure this out.

"How long do I have?" I asked.

"They want her out now," she said.

"She almost died a few minutes ago," I said. "Give her time to stabilize while I make other arrangements."

"You have a month," said Alexi.

CHAPTER 4

Change is inevitable, but I'm no different than most people who fear and resist it. Maturity is defined by a man's willingness to take full responsibility for his life. Blaming other people for our problems is immature and leads to a miserable existence.

It was time to make some changes in my life, beginning with taking care of Mom. The only way I can effectively do that is find a way to pay my debts. As a starting point, I need to use the win in Goth's high profile case to leverage a bigger paycheck, so I headed straight to the office to discuss it with John.

Unfortunately, his office was empty and didn't want to put this off another day since Shady Days didn't leave me much time. I considered picking up the phone, but if John didn't answer, then I would have to leave a message and I wanted to discuss this face-to-face without giving him a chance to prepare. John works late every day, and since it was still early, I figured I could catch him before he left for the day.

I decided to wait in my office until he returned and was surprised to find a bottle of the rarest bourbon in Kentucky sitting on my desk with a note of gratitude from Goth. It's like liquid gold if you're lucky enough to get your hands on it. They distill it in a batch so small it's damn near impossible to get unless you have serious money and connections. I had neither.

As I stared at the bottle, a call came in from Eric. We've been friends for as long as I can remember, but it was rare for him to call in the middle of the work day.

"Hey, what's up," I said.

"Dude, I can tell you are stone sober," he said. "There is no possible excuse you can give for not celebrating right now."

"It's not five o'clock yet," I said.

"Winners get a pass on that stupid five o'clock rule," he said.

"How did you know we won?" I asked.

"It's all over the news, including you running from the camera like you're afraid of it, or something," said Eric.

When I left for Shady Days, I found Goth talking to the press on the courthouse steps. He tried to wave me over, but I told him I had a personal emergency to tend to.

"I had somewhere else I had I be," I said.

"Why would you pass an opportunity like

that…didn't they teach you anything in law school about the power of free publicity?" asked Eric.

Instead of answering his question, I asked one of my own, "What's the press saying about the trial?"

"That you're a rising star who just won the biggest trial of the year," answered Eric.

"I don't know about that," I said. "What about that double murder trial a few months back?"

"Pathetic," said Eric.

"Look I'm just saying," I said.

"How did I end up with such a lame best friend?" asked Eric.

He paused to take a swig of whatever he was drinking, but not long enough for me to answer.

"Everybody knows a celebrity trial trumps double murder," said Eric. "Besides your little dog and pony show included twelve deaths. Goth is practically a serial killer and you got him off scot-free. Damn, I've never been more proud of you."

Eric's ramblings were intended to be funny, but after watching Mom fight for her life, they hit a raw nerve and I needed to change the subject.

"Something has happened," I said.

"Damn right something has happened," said Eric. "Get your butt over here and have a celebratory drink with me."

"Yeah, umm…I got something important to take care of first," I said.

"Geez, you're hopeless," said Eric. "I'll expect you in an hour. Anything longer and I will personally hunt you down and drag you to a good time."

"Ummm…okay," I said.

"This is important, Grant," said Eric. "You have to get better at celebrating the good things in your life and this one is epic. Don't you dare let this slip away without paying homage to the gods of victory."

The call dropped without another word.

Eric is right. It's time to celebrate. I broke the seal on the bourbon and poured myself a drink. You don't rush twenty three year old bourbon, so I swirled the glass and watched the amber liquid roll along its sides. Next, I warmed it with both hands before sticking my nose over the rim and inhaling deeply. I enjoyed the distinctive scent of the oak barrel. It smelled a little like caramel to me. There was another scent that was a little more difficult to identify, maybe vanilla.

Finally, I sipped just enough to cover my tongue and left it there for a moment before letting it roll down my throat. The bourbon was smooth…both soft and full-bodied. I let out a contented sigh.

Today's victory would be the first of many. In the meantime, I would develop a winning campaign to convince Shady Days to keep Mom. It's the only home she's known for the last twenty years and I don't want her to start over in a new facility.

As I mellowed with the drink, I stretched my legs and brought my feet to rest on the desk. It was at that very moment John appeared in the doorway.

He sniffed the air and said, "Your office smells like cheap booze. Are you drunk?"

His comment took me completely off guard. I had a bad feeling about the direction of this conversation and shifted slightly in my chair.

"Umm...no, of course not" I said. "I just poured one...but...umm...no, I'm not drunk."

John suddenly seemed angry and cut me off.

"This is not acceptable behavior for an attorney in this firm," said John. "I have to say that I'm extremely disappointed in you."

"It's just a celebratory drink," I said.

"If you had bothered to read the HR manual, then you would know that there is a zero tolerance for drugs and alcohol on the premises," said John.

I sat the whisky on the edge of desk, but when I dropped my feet to the floor the drink tumbled into my lap. There wasn't much left anyway, so I just left it. I was more concerned about John. His attitude was annoying and to control the rising irritation, I took a long and deep breath. It helped

Ch'ing says irritation ages us and if it becomes chronic, then it kills us. He taught me to relax in a difficult situation.

"Take a deep breath," Ch'ing had said. "Breathe all the way down to your toes. If you can learn to do that, then your irritation will evaporate."

Ch'ing is a martial arts teacher who appeared out of nowhere the day of my parent's motorcycle crash. You might say he helped shaped me into the man I've become. John was behaving like a bully and Ch'ing taught me to show a bully polite respect, but never fear.

"Sorry about that," I said. "It's a gift from Goth."

"You mean a gift from Mr. Goth, don't you," he snapped.

A uniformed officer appeared in the doorway next to John and asked, "Which one of you is Grant Li?"

"I am," I answered.

He handed me a summons and said, "You've been served."

It was a petition for dissolution of marriage. I moved out a couple of months earlier when my wife told me she was in love with another woman. I held out hope that we would find a solution to this problem. Clearly, she saw things differently and was headed in another direction. This was the end of a short and painful marriage.

Most guys that know about her sexual orientation snicker behind my back, like I'm not man enough to satisfy her. Or worse, they ask if I ever got a chance to be with the two of them. When I tell them no, I didn't even know it was going on, they quietly shake their heads, like I'm even less of a man because of that too.

John was red faced, "Somebody has served you with papers in this office."

"My wife," I said. "It's a divorce petition."

He rolled his eyes.

My mobile rang. I checked to see if it was Dr. Michaels calling with an update on Mom, but it was Eric. I declined the call and silenced the ringer so there wouldn't be any further interruptions. John glared at me, but said nothing about the call. Instead he went on the attack about the trial.

"Explain to me why I heard about the outcome of a trial involving this firm's biggest client on the news instead of from you," he said.

"I had a call from Mom's nursing home," I said.

"When?" he asked.

"While we were waiting for the verdict," I answered.

"You took a personal call in the presence of a client while in court," he said.

"Ummm, yeah I guess I did," I answered.

"You guess," he said.

"I did," I said.

John's scowl was growing.

"We expect more professionalism from our attorneys than that," he barked.

"It was an emergency," I said.

"Your personal life is a shambles and it's beginning to affect your judgment," said John.

"How can you say that?" I demanded. "I've worked sixteen hour days, seven days a week for months on this case. If anything has suffered, it's been my personal life."

I detected an ever-so-slight shake of his head.

"That is the minimum effort necessary if you want to get ahead in this profession," said John.

"I won a favorable verdict for a high profile client in a case with national interest," I said. "How's that for getting ahead?"

"It was hardly a slam dunk, since you barely avoided a hung jury," said John.

"Maybe, but I won," I said.

"You won nothing," said John. "The firm won this case. Do you really think you could have done this alone...without the support of the firm and all of its resources?"

"Maybe so, but I was the guy Goth chose to be in court with him throughout the trial," I said.

"It was your first trial," said John. "What exactly did you do to earn the job?"

"Look, I don't know why Goth wants me, but he does and I won," I said. "Now we need to talk about my salary."

His lips tightened into a thin line as he said, "You already earn more than any other young attorney with your level of experience."

"That may be, but I have bills I can't pay without a raise," I said. "I want my salary doubled."

"Doubled?" said John.

I nodded.

John went on the attack once again.

"I think you overestimate your value to this firm," he said.

"What do you mean?" I asked.

"You are a worker bee," he said.

I ignored an incoming text message from Eric and wished I could ignore the implications of what John had just said.

"Excuse me," I said. "I'm not sure what you mean by that."

"Each year we hire a group of young attorneys to increase our billables," he said.

"I don't understand," I said. "We work long

hours in the hopes of someday making partner."

"Have you noticed that most are gone before their one year anniversary with the firm?" said John.

I had noticed that and nodded.

"We don't intend to make any of you a partner," said John. "Instead, we pay you a small salary and then bill the clients for all of your long hours and hard work. We earn a huge profit off of your hard work and then wait for you to burn out. You drop like flies, but it makes no difference to us since there's plenty more young attorneys where you came from."

"That explains a lot," I said.

John shrugged.

"It's just good business," he said.

"Now I understand why you have been so upset that Goth insisted I handle his case," I said.

It was John's turn to nod his head.

"It would be disastrous if you lost the attorney Goth wants in his corner," I said.

John scowled at me, but said nothing. He was beginning to show signs that he was losing his composure.

"I guess that means I'm more than just a worker bee," I said.

"This law firm is a business," said John. "Pathogen accounts for 60% of our revenue stream. Our survival is tied to Pathogen and I will protect this firm at all costs."

"What are you saying?" I asked.

"I will not allow you to steal this firm's clients," said John.

"Who said anything about stealing clients?" I asked. "I just want a raise."

Helen appeared behind John in the doorway and said, "Mr. Biggs, you have a call."

"Take a message," said John.

"He says it's urgent," said Helen.

John glared at her and snapped, "Who says it's urgent?"

"Mr. Kruthers with the United States Attorney's Office," she said.

John whipped his head in my direction and asked, "Do you know what this is about, Grant?"

I shook my head.

"I'll take the call in my office," he said to Helen.

Eric messaged me to get my butt over there before he ran out of liquor. I wasn't ready to join him for a drink and didn't want to get into a debate with him about it, so I ignored the message and turned my phone off. The salary discussion with John was unresolved. I need that raise, and even though I promised Eric I would stop by for a victory drink, I wasn't leaving the office until John agreed to it.

I know a raise alone won't accomplish the goal

of keeping Mom at Shady Days without finding a way to convince the Board to give me another chance. If I could find the money to bring her account up to date, then I had a fighting chance, but it wasn't going to be easy.

Our assets are virtually non-existent. My wife collected credit cards like some women collect shoes. Every one of them is maxed out and I'm way too young to have amassed any significant retirement. I have nothing of value to sell. All I have is my law degree and a willingness to work hard.

Then it occurred to me, I had one other asset. I had Goth. I poured myself another glass of the whisky, and this time, I defiantly threw it back like it was rock gut. Once the burning in my throat subsided, I mindfully folded the divorce papers and then stuffed them into my hip pocket. I figured it was where they belonged...right there with all the other crap.

I headed down the hall in search of a raise. I didn't see John, but I did pass Richard and Laurie in the hall debating who had the worse parents. Like typical teenagers, they ignored me. When I turned back to say something to them about their rude behavior, I crashed into a short, balding man wearing an Italian designer suit that must have set him back at least eight grand. He went sliding across the marble floor like an air hockey puck before coming to a rest in front of John's office.

Richard and Laurie were snickering behind me as I helped Mr. Suit to his feet and offered my apologies. He glared at the giggling teenagers and then rushed off toward the main entrance with the kids strolling casually behind him.

John's door was ajar and I reached out to knock, when I first sensed something was terribly wrong. There was an odd gurgling sound coming from inside his office, but it was the smell of urine and feces that stopped me dead in my tracks.

I cautiously peered around the corner and into the room. John was dangling by the neck from a hideous fleur-de-lis chandelier in the center of the room. His swollen tongue protruded from a face bloated with blood that couldn't escape because of the knotted red power tie squeezing tightly against his jugular vein. His limbs convulsed one last time before he went deadly still.

Hoping the loud crack wasn't what I thought it was, I rushed to release him from the gallows. Once I had him on the floor, I fumbled to loosen the knot and then checked his pulse. I didn't feel one, but since I'm not trained for that, doubt filled my mind. Maybe he was still alive.

"Why did you do this to yourself?" I asked.

John didn't answer. Instead, I heard a shrill scream coming from the doorway. It was his secretary, Helen. She held her cheeks in hand and released a second scream.

I turned toward her with an extended hand and said, "Call 9-1-1."

Helen dug her cell out of a pocket and called the police, but instead of requesting an ambulance, she repeatedly stabbed an accusatory finger at me and told them that John had been murdered.

She looked at me with hate-filled eyes and said, "They're coming for you."

"What have you done?" I said.

"I hope you get the electric chair for this," spate Helen with more venom then I ever imagined she had inside of her.

I should have stayed and sorted this out with the police, but I had already been through so much in the last few hours. My nerves were raw. Bile was threatening to come up and I couldn't stop my hands from shaking.

I needed time to think and regroup. I told myself I was doing the right thing under the circumstances as I scrambled for the door, but I knew I was lying to myself.

CHAPTER 5

Friends provide insight and comfort in a crisis. I definitely needed some of that, as well as the drink Eric offered earlier, so I headed to his house. He lives to the east of Louisville, in Prospect, an affluent community overlooking the Ohio River.

Most of the residents work as professionals in Louisville. Each evening they endure rush hour traffic to escape to the quiet comfort of home and family. Most take pride in their homes and are known to gossip about a poorly tended lawn.

They drive luxury cars like Mercedes, Lexus, and BMW. Dad's old Ford doesn't fit in with all of the fancy imports, but no one ever seems to pay it much mind. They probably assume it belongs to a handyman hired by one of the neighbors.

I don't remember much about the drive. I was still in shock over the disastrous turn of events and must have been a couple of blocks past Eric's house before I realized there weren't any parking spaces on the street. Homeowners in this neighborhood have big garages to park their vehicles and these quiet suburban streets are usually empty. I scoured the area and was lucky enough to find a space two and a half blocks away I could squeeze into.

As I approached his house on foot, I noticed music was blasting from out back. Figuring I'd find Eric near the music, I followed it to the rear of the house and opened the eight foot privacy gate. The place was packed.

Eric's back yard is designed for entertaining. Every inch is utilized as living space with curved paths, fountains, koi ponds, and various sitting areas situated around the yard. Each area has a different theme. There are areas designed as a Zen garden, tropical beach, backwoods campfire, and Parisian café, among others.

Standing at the edge of the swimming pool was an exquisitely shaped brunette with The Eye of Providence tattooed on her lower back. I couldn't see the front, but her backside was flawless in a Barbie Doll sort of way. She wore one of those flesh toned bikinis that give the illusion of nudity. It did a wonderful job of complementing her figure. Her flawless legs lead the eye upward toward a tight little behind, while waves of soft dark brown hair fall gracefully onto her broad swimmer's shoulders.

As if the eye couldn't possibly convey all that she is, her musical laughter sliced through the party chatter and found its way to a dusty room deep in my mind where long forgotten memories were laid to rest. It was disconcerting.

I reluctantly pulled my eyes from the woman and appraised her companion. He was a few inches taller than her and several shades darker. Whereas her skin tone was olive, he was chocolate. His frame was packed with tightly compacted muscle that rippled in unison with their flirtatious back-and-forth banter.

He touched her lightly on the arm and flashed an eye-crinkling smile just before leaning in to whisper something in her ear. She pushed him away, but softened the rejection with a light-hearted laugh that, once again, sounded strangely familiar.

He answered the laugh with flared nostrils and a gentle push of his own. She rolled with it and counter-grabbed his upper arm in a surprising move that unbalanced him. He managed to drag her with him as the two of them tumbled into the water, making a huge splash that reached a group relaxing in lounge chairs.

When they surfaced, I saw her face for the first time. I couldn't believe it was Ginny, and found myself torn between the urge to run away and a strange need to watch her every move. Once again, he leaned in to whisper something to her, but her eyes suddenly opened wide in alarm. She had caught sight of me for the first time.

She let out a little squeak before pushing him away and scrambling from the pool. Once out of the water, she looked wildly about for a towel, before giving up and turning for the house.

Her flight was interrupted when a throaty voice called to her, "Are you okay, Ginny?"

Eric's wife, Kinsey, rose from a white wicker chair and walked toward her. She is tall like Eric and thin as a model. In fact, she did a short stint of modeling in New York before returning home to marry Eric.

If it wasn't for the boob job, her most prominent feature would be her large boney joints. She picked-up the boobs in New York and likes to refer to them as evidence of her misspent youth. Her strawberry blond hair frames a long face filled with freckles.

She is one of those people who could easily slide into unattractiveness, but has always made the most of what she has. Kinsey owns her sensuality, and because of it, she turns heads when she walks into a room.

It was the first time I had seen Ginny since high school. It had been ten long years and I couldn't stop looking at her. Once an awkward plain-jane, she had grown into a beautiful woman.

Ginny has an aristocratic high bridged nose set

between wide cheekbones. Her slightly flushed face narrows into a high forehead. I even spotted a few freckles on her broad shoulders. Believe it or not, the eyes are her best feature. They are the color of a tropical sea and filled with intelligence.

Of all the people I could have seen after a crazy day filled with anxiety and change, none would have been better for my spirits than Ginny. A page had indeed turned and the new chapter held more promise than I could ever have imagined.

She stopped in her tracks at the sound of Kinsey's voice, but did not change directions. Her body was still pointed toward the house when she glanced backward over a shoulder. Her eyes darted in my direction before quickly returning to Kinsey. Clearly, she was torn. Exhaling, she finally gave up her escape and turned in Kinsey's direction, but not before she flashed a hard defiant look at me.

Her decision had been made. There was something new in her eyes. It was grit. This wasn't the same awkward teenager from my past. Ginny had grown into a strong young woman.

Kinsey looked at me and frowned before repeating her question, "Is everything okay, Ginny?"

She looked like she was about to answer her old friend, but I cut her off.

"Ginny," I said.

It was hardly more than a whisper, but she heard me. Her eyes softened as she took a tentative step in my direction. I was equally timid as I matched her step. She was unsure of herself and it was my fault because I had ignored her for years. It was on me to close the gap between us, and if possible, repair what had been broken.

I took another step and then another. Before I knew it, we stood toe-to-toe on a strange new battlefield. I reached out and brushed aside a rebellious curl that had fallen across her face and was dripping water in a steady stream along the inside curve of her cheek.

She parted her lips and instead of speaking, she licked the last errant drop as it rolled past the corner of her mouth. I don't know why, but that simple act opened a conduit to my inner smile. It first came out as a contented sigh, but then grew into a full-blown smile, eyes and all.

The smile was contagious and spread wide across Ginny's face and deep into that place which is only revealed in the eyes.

"Hello, Grant," said Ginny.

"It feels really good to see you again," I said.

"Yes, it does feel good," she agreed.

"God, I've missed you," I said.

Ginny inhaled sharply and looked like she was about to say something, but was interrupted by

Eric.

"Well, well, well…if it isn't the man of the hour with a beautiful woman," said Eric.

I glanced over my shoulder and the first thing I noticed was a cheesy gold chain hanging around his muscular neck. If he wanted attention, it was working. The chain looked like something you'd see in a 1970's disco.

Eric is tall, lean, and well proportioned. I'm a couple of inches shorter than Eric and more muscular. My face, hands, and body are square. His blond hair and blue eyed Viking good looks drive chicks crazy. Not that they don't love my brown almond eyes and dark hair. At the moment, Eric's eyes were glued to Ginny.

"Welcome to the victory party," said Eric.

"Who are all these people?" I asked.

"Just fifty of your closest friends," said Eric with a grin.

"Right, I haven't seen half of them since high school and the other half I definitely don't know," I said.

"Dude, you work all the time," said Eric. "That doesn't leave a lot of time for nurturing friendships. I had to dig deep."

Kinsey spoke up and said, "Babe, Ginny's here!"

Eric's phone rang. He ignored it. Instead, he looked at Ginny and poured the charm on.

"Wow!" said Eric. "How did I miss you coming in...it's a pleasure to have you back in town."

Eric was on a roll.

Instead of waiting for an answer, he pointed toward me and said, "I take it you're not with this scoundrel. Good thing too! Grant, you remember Ginny from high school. She went away to college in California and then skyrocketed in the fashion industry as a designer. She and Kinsey have stayed in touch all this time, but this is the first time since graduation she has returned to Louisville."

Ginny visibly stiffened and narrowed her eyes to tiny slits. High school had been painful for her. I was surprised she had changed so much. In high school she was Kinsey's nerdy best friend, Virginia. She wore thick glasses and hardly ever spoke. Her hair was always pulled tightly back into a severe bun. Her clothes hung loosely on her without showing any sign she was making the transition from child to woman.

Throughout high school, I felt a strange mix of mortification and longing whenever I was near Ginny, so I avoided her at all costs and never spoke to her. Not even our best friends knew the reason why I behaved this way or the painful secret we shared.

I was trying to think of something to say to

make her feel better when someone put hands over my eyes and whispered, "Guess who?"

Geez, I knew immediately who it was…Cindy, the cheerleader I dated off and on throughout high school. What was she doing here? It was like a class reunion!

Instead of answering her question, I reached up and peeled her hands off. She slipped around and positioned herself between me and Ginny.

"Congratulations, Grant," she said. "You've become an instant celebrity. Look at all these people who came tonight just to rub elbows with the likes of you and here I thought you would never amount to much of anything at all. Nothing like winning your first case for a rich client to get your name all over the news. Although, seeing you run from the camera was just priceless."

Cindy got all of that out without taking a single breath. I figured she had been rehearsing it in her head for hours.

Ginny was a head taller than Cindy, who couldn't have been more than 5'2". I looked over the top of Cindy's blond head and into Ginny's hard gaze. This couldn't have been more awkward.

I thought it would be easier to look at Cindy instead of Ginny, but when I turned my attention back to my ex-girlfriend, she was looking at me like I was food and she was ravenously hungry. She was still cute as a button in a Betty Boop sort of way, with bright blue eyes, a little upturned nose, and girlish features that belied her real age, but I had zero interest in her.

"God, don't you look yummy," said Cindy.

Did she really think I was going to respond to that? I figured it was time to nip this one in the bud.

"We're having a private conversation here, so do you mind giving us some privacy, Cindy?" I said.

Cindy's expression shifted from her best cheerleader smile to an unpleasant scowl in an instant. She cut her eyes to Eric, but all she got from him was a shrug.

Her eyes narrowed for the briefest moment before she caught herself and rolled them upward along with both hands, palms facing the sky, like a snarky little teeny bopper.

"Try not to suck all the joy out of your little victory party, Grant," said Cindy. "You never know, it may be your last one."

She laid a hand on Ginny's arm and said with an exaggerated shake of her head, "Good luck with that girlfriend."

Ginny's eyes flared, "I'm not your girlfriend."

Cindy ignored her and was already off flirting with the nearest cute guy. Ginny looked like she wanted to pull every last hair out of Cindy's head.

Eric shook his head at Cindy and silently mouthed the word "chicks."

Kinsey gave Ginny a big hug, "I'm so glad you're here. Now, let's go inside and find you a towel."

We watched them scurry off to the house. Eric turned his attention back to me and frowned.

"Dude, you don't look like someone who is on top of the world," said Eric.

"A lot has happened since the verdict," I said.

"Let's go inside and get you a drink," he said.

"Yeah, I need one," I said

"Geez, we'll make it a double of my very best and then you can tell me all about it," he said.

CHAPTER 6

Kinsey insists on buying local, so the party was stocked with beer, wine and bourbon from the region. Eric poured a half tumbler of bourbon from a new Louisville distiller, dropped a couple of ice cubes in it, and then gave it a swirl before shoving it into my hand with a bottoms up command.

He was sipping from a bottle of beer. The company was established in 1905 by a group of entrepreneurs who banded together to fight a monopoly that had a strangle hold on the beer market in Louisville. Eric loves David and Goliath stories. It has become a tradition for him to repeat, "Go little guy," whenever he opens a beer, and this night was no exception.

"Are you trying to get me drunk?" I asked.

"Yep, you got a problem with that?" he said.

I shook my head, but said, "I'm not that kind of girl."

"You mind if us girls join you," asked Kinsey.

She and Ginny had slipped up behind us carrying two bottles of a Sauvignon Blanc from an area winery. Kinsey poured Ginny a glass of wine, which she immediately turned up and emptied.

Eric raised an eyebrow and quipped, "I didn't know we were doing shots."

"I'm just trying to relax," said Ginny.

"Girl, you keep that up and everyone will be stepping over your relaxed self in the middle of my kitchen floor," said Eric.

"I have a big day tomorrow, maybe I should slow down a bit," agreed Ginny.

He grabbed a couple of bottles of beer and the bourbon before heading out back where we settled into comfortable eco-friendly chairs arranged around a fire pit. Eric took a swig of beer and let out a belch that would have made any ten year old proud.

Kinsey rolled her eyes, but said nothing about her husband's social lapse. It may have been the wine going to her head, but Ginny giggled.

"Now that I've restored peace and stability to my gut, tell us what happened today to spoil your shining moment," said Eric.

I felt suddenly shy around Ginny and wasn't happy about revealing my problems to her. My eyes darted in her direction and then to my feet that were restlessly shifting back-and-forth at the foot of my chair.

Ginny looked incredibly sad as she said, "I'll leave if you prefer."

That was the last thing I wanted, so I sat up straight and then leaned in toward her as I said, "Please don't leave. I just don't want you to think…"

I couldn't say it out loud, but Cindy was right about one thing. In my finest hour, I was a failure.

"Whatever it is, Grant, it won't change my opinion of you," said Ginny.

"That I'm a jerk, who treated you badly," I said.

"No, I don't think that at all," she said.

I was relieved she didn't feel that way about me. Ginny had my attention now, so I leaned in a little closer and looked into her eyes for any sign of deception.

"Then what is it you think of me?" I asked.

"I think you are destined for greatness," said Ginny.

I was like man dying of thirst who fell upon an oasis in the desert. My wife, Cynthia, tortured me with her criticisms. I don't believe she thought I deserved to be anything more that a low level nobody. Hearing Ginny's words of encouragement refreshed my dying self-esteem.

I wanted to hug and thank her for what she had just given me, except we were interrupted by an old teammate from our high school football team, Jerry Flayer. The last ten years had aged him twenty. He looked beaten, as if life had slapped him around and then dared him to hang around for more.

"Hey Grant, I just wanted to congratulate you before I left," he said.

"Ummm, thanks Jerry," I said.

He reached across his face and absent-mindedly scratched his jaw line just below the ear. Jerry looked like he had more to say and wasn't certain if he should. Whatever it was, I doubted I was going to like it much, but waited for it, all the same.

"I've got to tell you old friend that I have mixed feelings about this," said Jerry.

"Why's that?" I asked.

"I don't know if you heard, but I lost my sister last year," he said.

"Yes, I heard, Jerry, and I sorry for your loss," I said.

He chewed on the bottom of his lip for a moment before blurting out, "There was a medicine that might have saved her, but she couldn't afford it. It costs $1,700.00 per pill and she needed a lot of pills."

"I had no idea," I said. "Wasn't there any insurance?"

"She lost it a couple of years back," answered Jerry.

"I'm sorry," I said.

"Here's the rub," said Jerry. "Six months before she got sick, the medicine cost eight dollars apiece. Then Pathogen bought the exclusive rights and increased the price."

I nearly spit out a sip of whiskey. It took a moment before I got it under control enough to speak.

"Pathogen?" I asked.

Jerry nodded. That simple action seemed to open a floodgate of emotion.

"They ki...ki...killed my sister with their greed," he choked out between sobs.

Ginny popped up and gave Jerry a comforting hug as he sobbed on her shoulder. The rest of us followed her lead and did the best we could to comfort an old friend.

He wiped the tears on the back of his hand and with big sad eyes said, "I'm happy for you, but I hate those people. Maybe you're fighting on the wrong side of this war."

After Jerry left, we sat together in silence for a few minutes. The quiet moment was broken by Eric's phone. Instead of answering the call, he grabbed the bottle of wine and leaned over to refill Ginny's glass, spilling the last few drops. His hand was shaking and that's not something you see very often.

Kinsey chewed on her lower lip as Eric sat back stiffly in his chair. They exchanged a glance.

Finally, Eric nodded slightly at Kinsey, who shifted her gaze to me. She took a deep breath and the corners of her mouth turned slightly upward just before she spoke.

"Grant, please don't take it personal, but we all know somebody who has been hurt by Pathogen," said Kinsey.

I slumped in my seat. The story about Jerry's sister had gotten under my skin and I didn't know what to make of it.

Eric jumped in with exaggerated light heartedness and said, "Hey what can you do, right. It's the way of the world, so tell us about the rest of your day."

I hesitated.

Ginny placed a reassuring hand on my shoulder and said, "Please, Grant, we'll listen without judgment."

"Isn't that what friends are for?" added Kinsey.

Yes, that is exactly what friends are for, so I told them everything that had happened to me before arriving at the party. They sat and listened to the whole story without a single interruption.

"That's a lot to take in, Grant," said Kinsey.

"Dude, no wonder you aren't your usual sparkly self," said Eric.

"Me sparkly?" I said.

"Are you sure your boss killed himself and

wasn't murdered?" said Eric.

"Who would kill him?" I asked

"Well, according to his secretary, you," said Eric.

My best friend has moments when his humor is inappropriate and this was definitely one of them. Kinsey jumped in for damage control.

"We know you wouldn't do something like that, but the police will be questioning you about this, so you might want to give some thought to who would want John dead," said Kinsey.

"He's made a lot of enemies," I said.

"Did you see anything out of the ordinary?" asked Kinsey.

I shook my head, but then remembered the guy I knocked down in the hall, Mr. Suit.

"There's the guy I bumped into outside of John's office," I said.

"Have you ever seen him before?" asked Kinsey.

I shook my head.

"Do you think he killed your boss?" asked Eric.

I shrugged.

"Hanging someone in a busy law office doesn't sound like the best way to commit murder," said Kinsey.

"There's a good way?" I asked.

"The logistics are just too much of a

challenge," said Eric.

"Logistics…really, you sound like you plan murders all the time," I said.

"I mean, he was hanging from the chandelier," said Kinsey.

"Exactly, how would you get him up there without him screaming his head off loud enough to sound the alarm," said Eric.

"Suicide is far more likely," said Kinsey.

"Do you have any idea why he would want to kill himself?" asked Kinsey.

"Not a clue," I answered.

"Did he seem depressed?" asked Eric.

"No, he was his usual arrogant self," I answered.

Ginny had been quiet during the discussion about John and we all were a bit startled when she spoke.

"Have you heard back from your mom's doctor?" asked Ginny.

"No, I haven't," I answered.

"You think her episode today was caused by this drug manufactured by Pathogen," said Ginny.

I nodded.

"It was the same exact symptoms discussed in Court," I said.

"Could it be something else?" she asked.

I shrugged.

"They're running tests on her and may know something more when the results come in," I said.

"Will the results be in before she…umm…before she leaves the facility?" asked Ginny.

"I don't know," I answered. "Her doctor didn't say how long it will take to get the results back."

"I haven't heard one word of blame from you," said Ginny.

"It's on me to find a solution," I said. "Blame is for control freaks and the immature."

"Isn't that sort of what lawyers do…play the blame game?" asked Kinsey.

"Blaming somebody else for our problems has never made much sense to me," I said.

"So, what are you going to do about it?" said Ginny.

"I need to make some changes, but I'm still trying to figure that out," I answered."

"Ummm, one more thing, Grant," said Ginny.

"What is it?" I asked.

"How do you feel about the divorce?" she asked.

I searched her eyes for some clue as to the reason she asked the question, but all I saw was someone who was worried about me.

"Relieved," I said. "I feel like I'm finally

waking from a really bad nightmare."

CHAPTER 7

Kinsey's eyes darted back and forth between me and Ginny. She looked like there was something she desperately wanted to say, but couldn't get it out. So instead she squeezed Eric's hand hard enough he winched and only managed to escape her clutches when his phone rang.

He excused himself, and as he walked away, we heard him say, "This better be important."

"Whatever it is, just go ahead and say it, Kinsey," said Ginny.

"What happened between you two that has made you act like fools toward each other all these years?" asked Kinsey.

It was the last thing I wanted to talk about, but maybe Kinsey was right. Maybe, just maybe, it was time to air it out.

"I've never told a soul," I said.

I looked at Ginny and what I saw in her eyes was a glimmer of hope. She gave me a nod, as if to encourage me to tell it.

I took a calming breath. Since I wasn't exactly sure where to begin, I pictured what happened in my mind all those years ago.

"It's one of my earliest memories, but I remember every detail like it happened yesterday," I said.

"We were just kids, maybe five years old," said Ginny.

"I'm not sure where to begin," I said.

"I find it's best to not overthink it," said Kinsey. "Begin your story with the first syllable that slides off your tongue and then let momentum take over."

That made sense to me, so I began just like that, and before I knew it, the telling transported me back in time…at least in my mind, anyway.

"It was a wild and unpredictable chase," I began. "Our prey suddenly changed directions and landed within reach. I stretched my tiny hand toward its powdery wings, but jerked to a stop when Ginny pleaded, "Don't scare it away, Grant."

We had chased it around the yard for the better part of an hour, giggling each time we had it cornered and then shouting when it made its escape. We were finally close enough to claim our victory and now she didn't want me to touch it. Geez!

I wanted to see what it felt like to hold it in my hand, but more than that, I didn't want to disappoint her. Not sure what to do, I shuffled my feet in the fresh cut grass. I could feel the blades between my toes, but not much on soles hardened from a summer of running barefoot throughout the neighborhood.

She gently squeezed my hand. I looked up from my grass stained feet and into her innocent eyes. They shifted between green and blue like a tropical sea. She was about my height, a little over three feet. She wore white shorts, a little pink top, and no shoes. Her dark hair was pulled back into a pony tail that dangled in soft curves to the middle of her back.

Her olive skin was tanned from the summer sun. She once told me the spattering of freckles on her nose and shoulders were a gift from her daddy. She was adorable and I was hopelessly in love with her.

Standing in a little patch of sun next to the creek, we watched the butterfly move from the flower to a cattail. Smiling she changed the subject. "Boys and girls are different," she said.

"Huh..," was all I said.

"Her eyes were big and innocent. "I saw a baby getting his stinky diaper changed," she said crinkling her nose. "He was different."

I had no idea what she was talking about. "Different," I said.

She pointed at the cattail and said, "Boy."

I said nothing, so she pointed at the flower

and said, "Girl."

She waited expectantly. I still didn't know what she was talking about.

"Oh silly, let me show you," she said.

Grabbing the elastic waistband, she yanked her shorts to her ankles and stepped out of them.

"Now your turn," she coaxed.

I shrugged and pulled my shorts down. She giggled and pointed. I looked down, but didn't see anything unusual.

A dark shadow loomed over us and something hard smacked me across the mouth, knocking me to the ground. I landed on a sharp stone and pain shot through my tailbone. Stars danced in front me as I gasped to catch a breath.

Two fat women loomed above me and then began moving together until there was just one. When I could finally breathe again, I gingerly touched my throbbing lip. I tasted something salty and saw blood on my finger.

The fat woman's lip was curled upward exposing yellow teeth. Her face got bigger and I felt a weight on my legs, pinning them to the ground. She planted her hands next to my ears.

I didn't like the look in her eyes, so I focused on a big vein throbbing in her neck. It made me think of the snake with big sharp teeth I saw on television the night before. I was pretty sure she had one crawling inside of her, and it scared me.

When she opened her mouth I expected it to crawl out and bite me. Instead, the pungent scent of garlic blasted me. I crinkled my nose. Yuck, I hate garlic.

"You nasty little boy," hissed the fat woman.

I was confused and scared but managed to mumble, "I don't know what you mean?"

She grabbed my ear and twisted it hard. "You're a nasty boy who can't keep his pants on," she said. "Outside even, where everyone can see. What's wrong with you, boy? Didn't your mother teach you anything?"

My ear hurt badly from the twisting she gave it and I desperately wanted the safety of my mother's arms.

"I think I hear my mother calling," I cried.

"So you're a liar as well," she said as she inched her face closer.

The movement shifted more weight to my legs and my knees were starting to hurt. I tried to squirm free but couldn't budge her. A wave of hopelessness washed over me.

"What do you want?" I asked.

"I'm going to make certain you never do this again," she hissed.

She even sounded like a snake. I shuddered.

"I didn't…I didn't do nothing," I said.

"Nothing…nothing, he says," she snarled. "You think hurting my little girl is nothing.

You're a nasty little boy like all the rest of them."

I didn't hurt Ginny. Maybe she thought I hurt the butterfly.

"I…I didn't…didn't hurt the butterfly," I stammered.

It didn't seem possible, but her face screwed up into a tighter ball of anger.

"You…you insolent little brat," she sputtered spraying a little garlic flavored spittle on my face.

I moved my hand to wipe the nasty stuff from my face, but she grabbed my wrist and slammed it back to the ground.

"How dare you raise a hand to me," she screamed. "I'm going to beat the devil out of you."

She raised a menacing hand to her ear and poised it for the first blow.

"Beat me," I said in voice that was barely audible.

Something warm and wet drizzled to the small of my back. The sour smell of pee was strong and I was afraid she would get even angrier if it got on her clothes.

"No…no please," I begged. "I didn't do nothing."

A small hand grasped the fat's woman's fist and I heard Ginny's voice plead, "Mama…mama, please don't hurt him."

Her mother's head whipped in Ginny's

direction.

"How dare you interfere with me," the fat woman said. "So you want to protect this nasty little boy. Then you'll get the first beating."

I was relieved when she climbed off me, but it was short lived as I watched her snap a limb from a tree and strip its branches. She ran her fingertips along its length and then shifted her attention to me.

Slowly her eyes traveled downward and stopped. The tip of her tongue moistened her lips. I didn't like the way she looked at me at all and reached for my pants, but they weren't at my ankles. Abruptly, she pulled her eyes from me and turned toward Ginny.

"Someday you will thank me for this," she said.

"Mama, please, don't," begged Ginny.

The corners of the Fat Lady's lips spread wide into a cruel smile.

"I'll beat the wickedness out you yet," she said.

With that, she tore into Ginny with a vengeance. It was brutal. Her screams pierced the quiet little neighborhood. The thing that scared me the most was the way her mother's smile got a little bigger with each blow.

I wanted to make her stop, but I couldn't move. I wanted to protect Ginny, but I was afraid the woman would turn the switch on me.

The best I was able to manage was to wrap my arms around my knees, as I rocked back and forth, whining in a voice only I could hear.

"Please stop," I pleaded.

"You'll not speak to that nasty little boy again," her mother hissed. "Do you understand me?"

"Yes mama," sobbed Ginny. "I promise."

My stomach was feeling hot and then I threw up all over myself. As I was wiping the vomit from my chin, the beating stopped, but not before angry red welts swelled across Ginny's backside.

Her mother was breathing heavy from the exertion. There was an odd glow to her face, as if she had enjoyed herself.

When she finally caught her breath, she said to Ginny, "Get your pants and go to your room while I deal with this nasty little half-breed."

"Yes, mama," said Ginny.

"When I'm finished here, I better find you on your knees in prayer," said her mother. "Say ten Hail Mary's and ten Our Father's as your penance. When you're done with that, beg God for forgiveness, and pray he does not to send you straight to eternal fire and brimstone for your sins."

Ginny nodded and then limped in the direction of her house. She only stopped and looked back once. Her eyes met mine. They looked so sad before she turned and disappeared into the house. I'm pretty sure it broke my heart, because I've never been able to truly love anyone else.

There wasn't any time for sadness that day. Terror washed through me when I tore my eyes from Ginny and looked into the body of hate that was her mother. Taking a menacing step toward me, she raised the switch.

I shrank from her and tried to make myself as small as I could. Closing my eyes, I waited for the first blow. Instead of the swish of the switch, I actually did hear my mother calling me for dinner.

Relieved that I hopefully wouldn't get the beating after all, I jumped up to run home, but she grabbed my arm and pulled me close and hissed.

"You think you've escaped your punishment," she said. "I'm sure you'll get much worse from your mother after I tell her about the terrible things you did today."

I tried to pull away, hoping the ordeal was over. It wasn't and my hope evaporated in an instant. The image of her beating Ginny flashed through my mind, and then was replaced with a picture of my mom standing over me with a switch. I felt a chill run up my spine and shuddered.

"Please don't tell Mom," I pleaded.

"The boy's afraid of his mother," she said. "That's good. I can use that."

She thought for a moment and then said, "If you don't want your mother to know her son is a nasty little boy, then you'll do exactly what I tell you. Is that understood?"

I didn't answer right away, so she squeezed my arm and glared at me. I wanted to tell her she was hurting me, but knew it would please her. Instead, I nodded my head.

"Promise you will never speak to my daughter again," said the Fat Lady.

I hesitated because that just wasn't something I could do. I loved being with Ginny. She was my best friend.

"Promise me," snapped her mother.

"Okay, okay, I promise," I said.

"If you ever come near my daughter again, I'll make sure your mother gives you the beating of your life," she said.

"I won't," I promised.

"May God have mercy on your miserable soul," she said.

With that she finally released me and I fled for home. I should have been happy I escaped without a beating, but I wasn't. I kept my promise, and never spoke to Ginny again…until today.

CHAPTER 8

My vision was turned inward toward the painful memory and it wasn't until I finished that I saw the tears streaming down Ginny's face. She gave me the strangest look, but said nothing.

"This explains a lot," said Kinsey. "You do know, Grant, that you can't spend your life victimized by the past. Especially something that happened when you were five years old. Ginny's mom caught the two of you playing a game of show-n-tell. Big deal, it's normal childhood curiosity. It certainly doesn't make you a bad person, or as she put it, a nasty little boy. I've met her mom, and no offense Ginny, but she is obviously the sick one."

I had never considered that her mother might be wrong. She had scared me half to death and I never wanted to feel that kind of terror again. So I did exactly what she told me to do, I stayed away from Ginny. Except, it didn't work.

"There's more," I said.

"What do you mean, more?" asked Kinsey.

"For months I had nightmares where I re-lived that horrible experience," I said. "I awoke every night to my own screams. Terrified, I refused to go back to sleep or to tell my parents the details of the nightmare for fear they would learn that it wasn't just a nightmare, that it really happened. They couldn't know I was a nasty little boy, because they might not want me anymore. The exhaustion caught up with us. At their wits end, they took me to see a doctor."

"Did it help?" asked Kinsey.

I shook my head.

"She was a bad person," I said. "She locked me in a hospital room and tortured me with electroshock treatments once a day for nearly a month."

"Oh, Grant," said Kinsey.

"I learned a lot from Sadistic Doctor," I said.

"What could you possible learn from that?" asked Kinsey.

"I learned to keep my nightmares to myself," I answered. "I learned to keep the screams inside. I learned to keep the people I love at a distance."

"I'm so sorry," said Ginny.

She looked like all of the guilt and shame buried deep inside of her had found its way to the surface. It hadn't occurred to me that her memories might also carry a load of negative emotion.

I started to tell her she had nothing to apologize for, but she abruptly got up and rushed into the house. I should have followed her, helped her, but I didn't. Instead, I just sat there and watched her walk away.

When I turned back to Kinsey, I saw a conflicted face. Her eyes shifted between compassion and anger. Without a word, she got up, gave me a hug and hurried after her friend.

I was alone.

The party continued all around me, but I didn't join in. Instead, I turned my attention inward...following the breath...relaxing tension wherever I found it...emptying myself, just like Ch'ing taught me.

I don't know how long I floated in the great void, but it was Eric's voice that pulled me out of the meditation. I opened my eyes and saw him standing on the deck in front of the French doors that lead into the rear of the house. His face was pale and drawn.

He waved toward the open door. I was halfway between the void and the real world, giving the scene an otherworldly hue. Like an autumn leaf, I caught the updraft from Eric's wave and floated past him into the house.

"My office," was all he said.

Eric keeps a small home office off the living room. While he has corporate offices nearby, he prefers to work remotely. Eric also likes to brag that he can run his company from anywhere in the world with a laptop and a cell phone. The truth is, while Eric works hard, Kinsey is the brains behind their success.

Following her modeling stint in New York, Kinsey returned to school. She attended the local community college for two years before enrolling at the University. After graduating with honors from a tough business program, she set out to build a first rate business.

At that time, Eric was working as a bouncer in a biker bar. Kinsey wanted more for them and it was her idea to start a security company. Thanks to her marketing skills, the business grew rapidly. Today, it is wildly successful and earns them a good living.

Eric closed the office door behind us. I settled into a comfortable oversized chair and watched quietly as he combed fingers through his blond hair. He didn't say anything for several minutes and then finally opened his mouth to speak, but stopped short. His hands were trembling.

"Something has happened," I said. "The phone...it was the call you took earlier. What has happened, Eric?"

"Ch'ing is missing," he answered.

Ch'ing has been our martial arts teacher and mentor since we were both eight years old. Calling him our teacher doesn't begin to describe the depth and reach of our relationship. He teaches us in the old way. Today, most dojos are businesses, but our relationship with Ch'ing is not a financial transaction.

We are tied together by bonds far greater than a tuition payment. It is a family bond that is stronger than any family I've ever been around. I couldn't imagine loosing Ch'ing.

"What do you mean…missing?" I asked.

"He didn't show up for class today," answered Eric.

To my knowledge, Ch'ing has never missed a class. He loves teaching, and as far as I know, has never been sick a day in his life.

"That's not possible," I said.

"I know," said Eric.

Ch'ing is eccentric. I wanted this to be just another oddity in the world of Ch'ing, but my gut wasn't buying this superficial explanation. I knew deep down that something very bad had happened to him, and I needed to help him.

Eric looked lost and afraid. I had never seen him like that and wanted to reassure him, but I felt fear in the pit of my stomach like nothing I've ever experienced.

"Have you tried to call him?" I asked.

"No answer," said Eric.

"Has anyone stopped by his house?" I asked.

"I sent one of my guys over," he answered.

I waited for him to tell me more, but he lost

his focus for a moment.

"What did he find?" I asked.

"Ch'ing's door was ajar," answered Eric. "The house has been trashed."

I couldn't imagine Ch'ing's house being trashed. His home is like a Zen garden with the elegance that flows naturally from simplicity. Everything has its place and is in perfect order at all times. More importantly, it is a peaceful retreat from the chaos of the outside world.

"Why would it be trashed?" I asked.

"There are signs that he was taken by force," said Eric.

This day was getting crazier and crazier. There's no way anybody could have taken Ch'ing by force. He's like superhuman or something. He is a martial arts master…the greatest that has ever been.

"There has to be some other explanation," I said.

Eric shrugged.

"Let's hope," said Eric. "In the meantime, the only way we'll get any answers is to find him."

Even though we had known him most of our lives, in many respects Ch'ing was still a mystery to us. Other than the monastery in Tibet, he never spoke of his past. He had appeared out of nowhere, and didn't seem to have any family that we knew of. Nor did he ever mention other people, let alone, any enemies.

"Did you call the police?" I asked.

He shook his head.

"You know how they are about missing persons," he said.

"I'll call Rose," I said. "Maybe she can help."

He nodded.

Rose is a detective with Louisville Metro Police Department. She and my Uncle Jim lived together when I was growing up, so she's like a second mother to me. She didn't take their breakup well and I can't have a conversation with her without listening to a monologue of complaints against Uncle Jim. I love them both and hate being in the middle of their problems.

Eric was looking lost and even though I was feeling like the biblical Job, I walked over to him and laid my hand on his shoulder. I stood toe-to-toe with him and held his gaze until he found himself again. I didn't step away until I could see in his eyes that he was back.

"We need to search his home," said Eric.

"I don't know if that's a good idea," I said.

"Most abductions end badly," said Eric. "There might not be much time left to find him."

"If you're right about the abduction, then his house is a crime scene," I said

"His house is the only place we have right now to look for clues," said Eric.

"Let me talk to Rose first," I said.

"You said that before," said Eric.

Eric knows me well and he knows that calling Rose wouldn't be easy for me.

"Call her now, Grant," said Eric.

I sighed.

Eric nodded.

He was right. This couldn't wait. It had to be done now. So, I dug into my pocket for the phone, but when I pulled it out the screen was blank. For a moment, I thought the battery was dead, but then I remembered turning it off at the office. I sighed once again and hit the power button.

When it booted up, I was surprised to see I had seven missed calls and eleven unread text messages. My impulse was to check the messages before I made the call, but Eric was growing restless, so instead, I dialed Rose's number and braced myself.

She didn't pick up, so I left her a voice message before hanging up.

"Let's give her a few minutes to call back," I said.

Eric grunted, but said nothing.

"Can you think of anyone else who might know where he is?" I asked.

"We can call around and talk to his other students," said Eric.

"Anyone else?" I asked.

He shook his head.

"Do you have a student list that we can divide up?" I asked.

Eric thought for a moment and then started toward his desk, when someone rapped on his office door.

"Come in," said Eric.

The door opened and a woman with the most beautiful chocolate complexion I had ever seen stepped inside. She gave me a little wave and then turned her attention to Eric. I didn't have a clue who she was.

"I'm sorry to intruded, but can I have a couple of minutes of your time," she asked Eric.

He looked like he might say no, but then thought better of it, and said instead, "What's on your mind, Ebonie?"

"There's a guy out by the pool who is creeping all the girls out," she said. "He's getting drunk and grabby. Do you mind saying something to him?"

Eric sighed.

"There's one at every party," he said. "Give me a minute to take care of this, Grant."

"Congratulations, Grant," said Ebonie.

She looked familiar and she seemed to know me, but I was having trouble placing her. It was her beautiful smile that I finally recognized, but she had changed. The young woman standing before me was half the size of the girl I knew in high school. Ebonie was now slim and fit.

"Thank you," I said. "By the way, whatever you're doing, keep it up. You look great."

"Thanks, but it's nothing," she said. "I discovered I like leafy green vegetables and the gym."

"I wouldn't call it nothing, because it's working," I said.

"Yeah, let's hear it for super foods," she said with a smile.

I followed them out of the office, but wasn't interested in Mr. Grabby. I knew Eric could handle it. Instead, I wanted to check on Ginny and make sure she was okay.

I expected to find her somewhere in the house with Kinsey, but didn't see her. I was thirsty, so I made my way into the kitchen to grab a bottled water. I had been monopolized by Eric, Kinsey and Ginny since I'd arrived at the party and now that I was standing alone in the kitchen I became a beacon for well-wishers wanting to congratulate me for my success in court.

When the last of them patted me on the back and finished telling me how happy they were for me, I let out a sigh of relief and thought again about Ginny. I wanted to make sure she was okay after re-living that terrible day so long ago.

The backside of Eric's house is a wall of glass that provides a view of the pool and yard. I glanced out the window and was surprised to see Ginny talking to some guy. I knew most of the people at the party, but not this one. He was good looking in a hippie sort of way, wearing jeans, sandals, and a Bob Marley t-shirt. His skin tone was brown, but the hair was blond and his eyes were blue. He wore his long hair pulled back into a ponytail.

Pony Tail leaned in and touched her arm to emphasize a point. I expected her to lean away from him, but she didn't. Instead, she threw her arms around him and held him tight.

I turned away from the spectacle she was making of herself and downed the water. Thinking I could use something stronger, I went in search of the bourbon when I ran into Kinsey.

There was still a touch of anger in her face, but mostly I saw concern.

"Are you okay, Grant?" she asked.

"Yeah, sure," I answered.

Her eyes softened a bit.

"That must have been really difficult for you," she said. "I saw how you looked at her earlier and it's exactly how you've always looked at her."

"If you're talking about Ginny, you're mistaken," I said.

Kinsey's eyes widened and then just as quickly

narrowed.

"What's this about, Grant?" asked Kinsey.

"She's like all the rest," I said with a touch of bitterness.

"The rest of what?" asked Kinsey with an edge to her voice.

"Women, the rest of the women," I said.

"You've had a bad day, Grant, and for the moment, I'm going to cut you just a little slack, since you've forgotten that I'm also a woman," said Kinsey.

She was right. It was a terrible generalization and I'm better than that...she's better than that.

I tried to apologize.

"I'm sorry, it's just..." I said.

"You're an idiot who doesn't know anything about women," said Kinsey.

"I know they can't be trusted," I snapped.

"Really, Grant, and why is that?" asked Kinsey.

"My wife for one...she cheated on me with another woman," I said.

"You married a lesbian and now you're shocked it didn't work out," said Kinsey. "Have you considered for a moment that embracing her true nature is the most honest thing she could have done, or, are you too caught up in your own drama?"

"You may be right about Cynthia, but that doesn't explain why Ginny is out there right now hanging all over some surfer dude," I said pointing over my shoulder.

Kinsey looked past me and said, "I don't see her."

I turned and looked out the window. Ginny was nowhere in sight.

"She was there a minute ago," I said.

"I don't know what you saw, but there is one thing I know beyond a shadow of a doubt," said Kinsey.

"What's that?" I demanded.

"Ginny loves you and she always has," said Kinsey.

CHAPTER 9

Ginny loves me. It doesn't seem possible considering the way I've treated her all these years. Kinsey must be mistaken. I was about to ask her if Ginny ever actually told her that she loved me, but we were interrupted by Eric.

"All right, the drunk with wandering hands turned out to be Kim Massinkil's date," said Eric. "It was their first. What do you think the odds are on a second date?"

"Is it under control?" asked Kinsey.

"He's sitting on the front porch waiting for a ride," answered Eric.

"While you grab Ch'ing's student list, I want to talk to Ginny for a few minutes," I said.

"No can do, Dude," said Eric.

"You don't have a list?" I asked.

"Yeah, I have a list, but talking to Ginny will be a challenge," said Eric.

"Why is that?" I asked.

"She left with a hippie dude," answered Eric.

I cut my eyes to Kinsey, but resisted the temptation to say I told you so. From the look on her face, I'd say she was using her powers of mental telepathy to shut her husband's mouth, but he wasn't listening.

"Let me guess, he had a Bahamas tan, blond ponytail and was wearing a Bob Marley t-shirt," I said.

Eric cleared his throat before answering, "Yeah, something like that. Is there a problem?"

"Nope," I answered.

Kinsey tried to step in and soften this latest news, "Grant, you shouldn't…"

I cut her off and said, "We have more important things to focus on right now, like finding Ch'ing."

"Has something happened to Ch'ing?" asked Kinsey.

"He's missing," said Eric.

"His place was busted up," I said.

"Have you heard back from Rose?" asked Eric.

"You called Rose?" asked Kinsey.

"Yes, I called Rose and no I haven't heard back from her," I answered.

As if on cue, my phone rang and it sent me pocket diving once again. It was the prosecutor, Zeke Kruthers, calling.

"Is it her?" asked Eric.

I shook my head.

"No, but I have to take it," I answered. "Can you grab that student list while I see what he wants?"

"Sure thing," said Eric. "Let's make some calls, Babe."

"Mr. Kruthers," I said.

"We need to talk," he said.

"I don't have my calendar with me," I said. "Can you call the office Monday morning to schedule an appointment?"

"This won't wait," he said. "Can you meet for a beer?"

"Umm, well, we kind of have an emergency here," I said.

"Whatever your emergency is, this will trump it," he said. "All I need from you is the time it takes to drink one beer."

"Are you buying?" I asked.

"Yeah, sure," he answered.

"Where did you have in mind?" I asked.

"Do you know Ed's Tavern down on the river?" he asked.

"The dive bar on Harrods Creek?" I asked.

"That's the one," he said. "Meet me there in fifteen."

I found Eric in his office and told him that I had to meet Kruthers for a few minutes, but would be back to help with the search for Ch'ing. The few stragglers at the party who hadn't congratulated me yet, caught me on the way out the door. I thanked them as quickly as I could without being rude and then I was on the road again.

My phone rang just as I pulled into the gravel parking lot of the bar. I would have let it go to voice mail, but it was Uncle Jim.

"Geez, I thought you were in jail or something," said Uncle Jim.

"Why would you think that?" I asked.

"Detective Lambers stopped by the house and was asking questions about you," said Uncle Jim. "Do you remember him?"

I remembered him all right. I had heard the story a million times, but had learned long ago it's best to go with it.

"Isn't he Rose's ex-husband?" I asked.

"Sure is," said Uncle Jim. "Can you believe it, he still holds a grudge because he thinks I stole Rose from him?"

I sighed. Here we go. When it comes to assigning blame for their busted relationship, Uncle Jim could be as bad as Rose when he gets on a roll. It's best to nip it in the bud, if I can.

"Unbelievable," I said. "Everybody knows Rose chose you because you're the better man. What did Lambers want?"

"Said he's working homicide these days," said Uncle Jim. "Who'd you kill, Son?"

I know it was intended to be a joke, but given the day I'd had, it didn't sit well with me.

"John Biggs hung himself today," I said.

"What do you mean, he hung himself?" asked Uncle Jim.

"I mean he tied the end of his red power tie onto the chandelier and kicked a chair supporting his feet halfway across the room," I answered.

"Geez, what would make him want to go and do a fool thing like that?" said Uncle Jim.

"Beats me," I said.

"You'd think he'd be happy and in a mood to celebrate following your big jury verdict," said Uncle Jim.

"You'd think," I agreed.

"Congratulations, by the way," said Uncle Jim.

"Thanks," I said.

"You don't sound too happy about winning your first big case," said Uncle Jim.

"I'm happy about the win," I said.

"Well, cheer up then," he said.

"I'm sorry, but it's been a tough day," I said.

"What else has happened that's big enough to tarnish your milestone victory?" he asked.

"Geez, where do I begin…umm…well let's see…Cynthia filed for divorce," I said.

There was dead silence. It lasted long enough I thought the call might have dropped, but Uncle Jim finally spoke again.

"How do you feel about it?" he asked.

"Happy to be moving on with my life," I

answered.

"That was a bad fit from the start," he said.

In my mind's eye, I could see him shaking his head as he said it.

"Yeah, she likes girls and I'm a boy," I said.

"Good riddance if you ask me," he said. "What has really got you upset, Son?"

"Shady Days is evicting Mom," I said.

"What?" said Uncle Jim. "I don't understand how they can do that."

"Cynthia has a spending problem," I said. "I'm broke and don't have the money to pay Shady Days."

"Spending problem…like I said, good riddance," said Uncle Jim. "Do you want me to drop by Shady Days and talk to Alexi about the bill?"

"No, I spoke with her earlier," I said. "I'll think of something."

"When do they want her out?" asked Uncle Jim.

"End of the month," I answered.

"Geez, that doesn't give us much time," he said.

Uncle Jim loves his sister and I know he'll do whatever he can to help, but a military pension hasn't exactly left him financially flush.

"Tell me about it," I said.

"Grant, I know you love your Mom and

wouldn't do anything to put her at risk," said Uncle Jim.

"I'll fix this," I said. "Did Lambers leave a card?"

"Yep, got it right here," answered Uncle Jim.

"Can you take a picture and text it to me?" I asked.

"Seriously," said Uncle Jim. "You want me to do what now?"

Uncle Jim hasn't wholeheartedly embraced the full line of features on his new smartphone. I needed to try something different.

"Can you text me the number?" I asked.

"And you will read it like all the other text messages I sent you today," he snarked.

I sighed. Uncle Jim gets testy when I don't respond immediately to his calls and messages.

"I turned my phone off earlier for a meeting and forgot to turn it back on," I said.

"Humph," said Uncle Jim.

"The number," I said.

"I'll text it to you," he said and hung up.

I figured it would be a while before I got the text, so I headed inside. Ed's Tavern isn't much more than a shack at water's edge. It's one of those neighborhood watering holes that owes its survival to outside customers. In this instance, it's a combination of bike nights and boater happy hours.

The boaters come in from a day on the river wearing swim suits and flip flops. The bikers enjoy the river views from the saddles of their motorcycles as they parade up and down River Road. Inside, they rub elbows with area residents and add their spending dollars to the locals hard earned paychecks.

The bar never changes. I'm pretty sure the last coat of paint was applied in the 1950's when the place first opened. It is dark and dirty on the inside, with maybe twenty-five tables jammed together in a space better suited for half that. Everyone else spills outside to sit at the worm eaten picnic tables and rusted-out cast iron tables dotting the riverbank.

I found Zeke sitting at a picnic table that was pulled off to the side and offered the greatest amount of privacy. I was accustomed to seeing him in a cheap government issued business suit, and it took a few before I spotted him wearing a pair of crisp new blue jeans and a canary yellow polo shirt.

He waved me over and pointed to a full bottle of beer sweating on the table. We shook hands and I sat in front of the beer.

"What's so important?" I asked.

His eyes darted around the crowd before he answered in a voice barely above a whisper.

"Keep it down, would you?" he said.

I nodded in response and couldn't help but think, how's this for keeping it down.

"Geez, Grant, what are you doing showing up in a place like this wearing a business suit?" he asked.

"I haven't been home yet," I said.

He shook his head and said, "One of the things I like about government work is we keep normal hours."

I absent-mindedly tapped the beer bottle, but I think he took it as a reminder he only had one beer to say his peace. I was actually thinking about the arguments my wife and I had over the long hours spent at the office.

"Long hours have their costs and rewards," I said.

"Congratulations, by the way," said Zeke. "I'm sorry I stormed out today without telling you that."

"Thanks, but I don't think that's why you called me here," I said.

He looked around again before speaking.

"Did you put that envelope on my table today?" he asked.

"No, I didn't," I answered.

"Look, if you did, I won't report you," he said.

"Report me to who and for what?" I asked.

"It's a game changer," he said.

"What are you talking about, Zeke?" I asked.

"I told you, the envelope," he answered.

"As I said, I didn't put it there, and if I did, I would say so," I said.

"All right, don't go postal on me," he said.

"What's in the envelope?" I asked.

"I can't tell you," he said.

"Then why did you bring it up?" I asked.

"Because it involves your client," he said.

"Goth?" I asked.

"Pathogen," he answered.

"In what way?" I asked.

"I can't tell you," he answered.

"Look this is going nowhere really fast and you asked for this meeting," I said.

"I was sure you left the envelope," said Zeke.

I opened my mouth to protest once again, but he held up his hand.

"If you had left it, then we could talk about the contents," said Zeke.

"What difference does that make?" I said.

"This complicates things," he said.

I wanted to know how it complicates things, but I was finally getting the picture that even though Zeke wanted to discuss it, he can't. I figured there had to be a legal or ethical barrier, that wouldn't exist if I was the source, but I couldn't imagine what it was.

"There's more," he said.

"Just get on with it and say what it is you want

to say," I said.

"It involves your law firm, particularly, John Biggs," he said.

I felt a chill run my spine.

"Did you speak to Biggs today?" I asked.

He nodded.

"What did you talk about?" I asked.

"The contents of the envelope," answered Zeke.

"Seriously, Zeke, if you could discuss it with John, then why not me?" I asked.

"Because it involves him directly," said Zeke.

It was time to shift the tone of the conversation.

"Did you know he hung himself?" I asked.

The blood drained from Zeke's face. When he spoke again, his hands were shaking.

"I didn't know he would go and kill himself," he said.

"What did you say to him that would cause him to hang himself?" I said.

"I told him there would be new indictments," he answered.

"For what?" I asked.

"I can't say," answered Zeke.

"What can you say?" I asked.

"Investigate your father's death," he said.

"What is that supposed to mean?" I asked.

"Look, I'm really sorry, but that's all I can

say," he said.

"Then we're done here," I said.

"Just one more thing, Grant," said Zeke.

"What?" I asked.

"I'm really scared of these people," he said.

"You're scared of who?" I asked.

"Watch your back, Grant," he said.

Zeke rose from the table and left without another word.

CHAPTER 10

I have to say, the entire conversation with Zeke baffled me. He was acting like he was genuinely spooked and I didn't have any idea what it was about, except it involved Pathogen and John Biggs.

Oh, and then there was that business about my father's death. That was twenty years ago and he was killed in a motorcycle wreck. What in the world could he be talking about?

I pulled my phone out to call Eric about Ch'ing and saw the messages and missed calls from earlier. Since I still had a half a beer I decided to take a few minutes to go through them.

The first voice message was from a partner at the law firm. It was short and to the point.

"Grant, this is Bill Pulver. In light of John Biggs' death, you should take a leave of absence until this matter is cleared up."

A leave of absence means no pay. I need that job to take care of Mom. What am I going to do now? I took a swig of beer and gazed out over the water hoping I might get the perfect answer in a flash of insight, but nothing came to my rescue.

The next voice message was from Uncle Jim. It was a no frills message.

"Call me," he said.

I took a draw off the beer and checked the time. It was earlier in the day and we've since spoken, so I listened to the next message. It was Roxanne from Shady Days.

"Grant, I'm leaving my shift and wanted to let you know that I've been with your mother all day," said Roxanne. "She's still not awake. Thoughts and prayers. Oh, one more thing. I heard about your trial. Congrats."

It meant a lot to me that Roxanne took the time to sit with Mom today and to give me an update. I know that isn't part of her job description. She did it because she's a good person and it's the right thing to do.

I didn't want Mom to be alone, but visiting hours were about up and I still needed to help Eric find Ch'ing. So, I promised myself I'd stop by tomorrow for a visit. I drank the last of the beer and slapped at a mosquito.

"Blood sucking vampire," I grumbled.

The next message was from Goth. It wasn't much.

"This is Wilbur Goth. I need to speak with you."

I figured I'd call him back later. Right now I had too much on my plate. There was a duplicate message from Uncle Jim to call and one from Eric demanding I come have a celebratory drink with my best friend. The final message was from Detective Lambers to call him regarding the death of John Biggs.

I slapped at another mosquito and started on the text messages. There wasn't much there. It was a bunch of call-me messages from Uncle Jim and Eric. I deleted them and was about to stuff the phone into my pocket, when it rang. It was Rose calling me back.

Caller ID has pretty much eliminated the old school tradition of saying hello and waiting for the caller to identify themselves.

"Hi Rose," I said.

"I heard about your verdict today," she said. "Congratulations."

"Thanks," I said.

"Your Uncle Jim must be very proud of you," said Rose. "I know I am."

Geez, here we go. I cleared my throat while I tried to think of a way to distract her from Uncle Jim. As it turned out, it wasn't necessary.

"You should be out celebrating with your friends and co-workers, instead of calling a washed-up old broad like me," said Rose

The washed-up old broad reference was a

slippery slope into fifteen minutes of what went wrong between her and Uncle Jim, so I ignored it, and instead, focused like a laser beam on the purpose of the call.

"Ch'ing is missing," I said. "We don't know how long he's been gone, but his place is torn apart and it's giving us the willies."

"Other than the condition of the place, is there any blood or other signs of violence?" she asked.

"I haven't gone through it yet," I answered. "We wanted to clear it with you first."

She exhaled loud enough I could hear it over the phone.

"Let's you and I have a look together," she said.

"I'm just leaving Ed's Tavern," I said. "I can meet you there in ten."

"It'll take me a few minutes longer," she said. "Don't go inside without me."

"Thanks, Rose," I said. "I'll see you there in a few."

I made one last call to Eric to let him know the plan.

"Dude, where are you?" he asked.

"I'm leaving Ed's Tavern now," I said.

"You're such a slacker," he said. "If I didn't know you better, I might think you let today's win go to your head."

"I may be sitting on the river bank, but I'm

not pulling a Huck Finn on you," I said.

"More like Tom Sawyer," he said. "You snookered me into making all the phone calls."

"Any luck?" I asked.

"No one knows anything about Ch'ing's whereabouts," said Eric. "Any luck with Rose?"

"She's on her way right now to meet us at Ch'ing's place," I said.

"That's what I'm talking about," said Eric. "I'll see you there in a few."

Ch'ing's home is upriver a couple of miles from Ed's Tavern. It's an old Victorian with attached bait shop. He meticulously restored the house from old photographs to its original glory and converted the bait shop into a dojo. The place comes complete with a boat ramp where he keeps his kayak and sailboat moored. Sometimes I think he confuses Louisville with Cape Cod.

I studied the mansion from one of the parking spaces in front of the dojo. Eric's men had pulled the front door shut, but I could see into the windows. Ch'ing doesn't use blinds or curtains to close out the light. His place is ordinarily full of life, but today it looked abandoned.

The wrap around covered porch extends the full length of both sides and the front of the house forming a horseshoe. Like many Victorians, it is asymmetrical with a four-story turret on the left and a three-story dormer on the right.

The siding is painted a medium shade of grey and the rust trim matches the slate roofing material. The decorative trim adds cream highlights to mix. There is no lawn to speak of. Instead, the lush yard is filled with a variety of mature trees, shrubs and colorful wild flowers.

It wasn't long before Eric pulled into the space next to me. He was driving a black paneled truck with the name of his company, Cotungin & Company Security Specialists, painted in orange script on the side.

Eric was wearing his combat face, jaw set tight and eyes unwavering. He loves to fight and I've watched many of his opponents falter when they face his ferocity for the first time. Still, it was highly unlikely he would see any action today.

Neither of us spoke. Instead, we sat quietly and watched the place for any sign of trouble. Rose arrived just as we both started to lose patience and began formulating mental excuses to justify going in without her.

"I can see I got here just in time," said Rose. "Another minute longer and the two of you would already be inside."

Rose knows us well. She gave both of us a big hug. Eric got an additional disapproving tsk for the length of his hair as she tugged at one of the sandy blond locks curled over his collar. Neither of us minded her mothering behavior and if the situation hadn't been so serious we might have enjoyed a little lighthearted back-and-forth banter.

She handed us disposable gloves and said, "Put these on, but refrain from touching anything until we have some idea about what's going on here."

We both nodded in agreement.

She led us to the big storefront window and had a look through the glass into the dojo. It appeared undisturbed, so we headed to front door of the house. There was no sign of forced entry.

Rose used her thumb and forefinger to turn the knob and push the door open. She stood in the doorway and scanned the room. Eric and I stood behind her, shifting our feet like a couple of racehorses loading the gate for a big stakes race.

Much to our dismay, she took her time surveying the room. We couldn't see a thing and knew better than to rush her. Instead, we had to settle for craning our necks in the hopes of catching a glimpse beyond the door.

Finally, she stepped inside and made room for us to follow, but held a hand up to slow our break from the gate. Taking her cue, we entered in our best ninja mode, slowly, with all five senses engaged.

The entry hall never fails to take my breath away. It is twenty feet wide and reaches the length of the house. At the far end is a large bay window overlooking the Ohio River.

To the right is a wide staircase made of polished mahogany that curves upward to the second floor. Matching mahogany wainscoting lines the lower half of the wall. Dark inlays in a triangular pattern form a border around the outer perimeter of the polished mahogany floor. Intricately carved columns lead into the western wing of the house.

The central table had been overturned and the area rug was cluttered with a spilled vase of white lilies that had been cut fresh when the day began. A message had been spray painted on the wall that read, "It has begun." Underneath the message was a symbol similar to an ouroboros, except instead of a snake swallowing its own tail, this was a snake and a bird forming a circle and swallowing each other's tail. An unfamiliar plant was painted on the rest of the wall.

"Have either of you seen this mural before?" asked Rose.

We shook our heads.

"It looks like gang graffiti," said Rose.

We slowly made our way through the

remaining rooms in the house. There was no blood. Nothing was broken, but Ch'ing's thing were scattered everywhere. The one thing that caught my eye was an old black and white photograph of Ch'ing standing outside of a monastery carved into the side of a cliff. It was lying in the middle of a mess of papers on his office floor. I had never seen it before.

"Do you think somebody took him?" asked Eric.

"The place has been vandalized, but I don't see any evidence of violence," said Rose. "If somebody tried to take him against this will, Ch'ing would put up a fight."

I swept my arm around the room, "You have to admit, this doesn't look good."

Rose shook her head.

"They could have broken in when he wasn't here," she said. "Did he mention a trip?"

"Kinsey and I have been calling his students and none of them know anything about his whereabouts," said Eric

"Is there anyone else?" she asked.

"I could ask Uncle Jim," I said.

Rose's face tightened, but she didn't start one of her tirades about him.

"Do you think they were searching for something?" I asked.

"That's possible," she said. "Can you tell if

anything is missing?"

We shook our heads.

"What can we do?" asked Eric.

"Keep asking around and calling his phone," she said. "I'll keep an eye out, but other than possibly filing a report for the vandalism, there's nothing I can do right now. If he doesn't show up in a few days, then we'll do a missing person."

"Thanks for helping," said Eric.

"There's one other thing," I said.

"What's that?" asked Rose.

"John Biggs hung himself today," I said.

"I heard," said Rose.

"Lambers wants to interview me about it," I said.

"That's news to me," said Rose.

"Do I need an attorney?" I asked.

"As an attorney you know the smart thing is to have representation at any interview where you are a person of interest," said Rose.

I nodded.

"Is there any doubt that it was a suicide?" asked Rose.

"Not in my mind, but John's secretary thinks different," I said.

"It's your call, Grant, but I'll see what I can find out for you," she said.

CHAPTER 11

Detective Lambers doesn't try to hide his dislike of Uncle Jim. Instead, he will tell anyone who is willing to listen. His tune sounds like the lyrics of a bad country and western song that goes something like, I hate him because he did me wrong.

I could wait for Rose to put out feelers with Lambers or I could consult with an attorney, but I didn't feel like waiting. On the heels of good fortune, this day had turned into something ugly. It would eventually turn again, but I didn't want to wait. Instead, I wanted to take constructive steps to resolve some of these problems and Detective Lambers seemed to be as good as any place to start.

Besides, I saw no value in making assumptions about his intentions. If I'm not careful, my mind will easily slip into a dark place that believes this hateful man is out to get me. I'm a twenty-first century Taoist and Ch'ing would never let me get away with such sloppy thinking.

Ch'ing focuses on the facts. He only considers data acquired directly from his senses and carves away any assumptions. One of his favorite internal arts is called Marrow Washing Chi Kung. While it has a physical component, the internal aspect of the practice contains the hidden secrets of the art. It is used to scrub the mind of self-deception. Ch'ing insists it is the shortest path to clarity.

I could certainly use a little clarity at the moment, so I returned Detective Lambers call. It went straight to voice mail. What now I thought to myself? The prospect of sitting alone in my little apartment didn't appeal to me. I had a moment where I wished I had taken Eric up on his offer of dinner, but dismissed it because I wasn't a bit hungry. While I awaited his return call, I needed to focus my attention on accomplishing another positive task.

My thoughts turned to the leave of absence from work. I didn't have any illusions about what it means. There was no longer a place for me at the firm. I had been let go. It didn't seem a bit fair to me, but then I had learned early on that lawyers don't care much about what seems fair.

Law schools flood the market each year with fresh eager faces hoping to make a mark for themselves. A young lawyer works long hours to get a toehold into the legal market. Being a lawyer may sound glamorous, but it's a competitive profession where you have to get your hands dirty to get ahead of the rest of the pack.

Attorneys learn to criticize everything, including each other. It creates a mindset that infiltrates our personal lives as well. I learned in my marriage it is not easy to sustain a relationship when you're busy attacking others. Most young lawyers give up the practice once they get a taste of these harsh realities, but it doesn't bother the law firms much since they have a steady supply of replacements.

I decided it was time to return to the office to pick up my personal belongings and headed that way. It was a little after nine when I pulled up to the building. We're on the thirty second floor and ordinarily there would be a few lights still shining through the windows, but on this night the office was dark and ominous.

I still had a key card to the building, but I wasn't sure if it worked. I had never been on a leave of absence before and a part of me felt like a thief sneaking into someone's home. The security camera pointing straight at my face didn't help relieve the angst I was feeling. My hand shook slightly as I slid the card into the slot for the garage overhead.

A wave of relief washed over me when the door began rising, but it turned to confusion when a car roared out and damn near side swiped me as soon as the door was high enough for it to pass through. They were obviously in a hurry. It didn't help my growing anxiety one bit, and I had to resist the temptation to just forget the whole thing and go home.

The garage was mostly empty. A lone car was parked in an area where the lights were burned out. It reminded me of a tombstone standing watch on a dark night. I was accustomed to leaving the building at a late hour, but being here under these circumstances was creepy. I managed to pull it together enough to slip the battered old truck into my assigned parking space.

I never lock the truck, because I figure no one would want to steal it, but this time, I did lock it. Stuffing the keys into my pocket, I headed toward the elevator, but stopped when I thought I heard someone calling out from the direction of the tombstone. When I turned toward the sound, there was no one there.

I changed my mind about taking the elevator and chose the stairs instead. I wanted to keep moving and being trapped in a box hanging from a cable did not appeal to me at the moment.

Since I was parked on lower level two, it was a thirty four story climb, but I had done it many times before as part of my training for mountain climbing trips out west. A busy lawyer has to find ways to incorporate fitness training into his daily routine if he hopes to stay on his game.

I hoped the physical exertion would help clear my spooked head. A sour smell in the stairwell door did little to alleviate my anxiety. I noticed a puddle of fresh urine with a faint hint of steam still rising from it. Why do people urinate in stairwells? I reconsidered the elevator, but couldn't get past the uneasiness I felt about it, and began the ascent.

It could have been the stress-filled day, but the climb seemed unusually difficult. I had to stop several times to rest. It might have been my imagination, but I thought I heard footsteps in the stairwell below. Each time I stopped the steps below continued like an extended echo before coming to an abrupt stop. Someone seemed to be following me and trying to avoid discovery.

The thought of someone stalking me was creepy enough, but under the circumstances, it was nerve wracking. Maybe I was being paranoid, but I kept thinking about Kruthers telling me he was afraid of these people. He was spooked and it spooked me. I had a few questions I wanted to ask this stalker, so I devised a strategy to catch whoever it was.

After climbing four more flights of stairs, I

opened the door leading to the twenty-fifth floor, but didn't step through the threshold. Instead, I quietly crept further up the stairs until I was out of view and waited. I expected the stalker to rush up the stairs, but that didn't happen. In fact, nothing happened at all.

It's possible that my pursuer didn't take the bait, but I convinced myself instead that the whole thing was nothing but my imagination. Chiding myself for getting spooked over nothing, I finished the climb and slipped into my old office. It is never a good idea to ignore our instincts and I would later wish I had listened to mine.

The office foyer is intended to impress. The marble flooring is polished to a high sheen. Matching Doric columns and a fresco of the Parthenon is calculated to give the impression that Socrates resides within its walls. To me, it's a little over the top. The first time I stepped into the place I half expected to see everyone dressed in togas and sandals.

Ordinarily, there are number of young attorneys working late on projects dumped on them at the last minute and a night shift of clerical staff working diligently to meet the next day's deadlines, but not on this night. On this night, the offices were all empty. As far as I could tell, there wasn't a soul working. Everyone was probably sent home in deference to John's death. The place felt like a mausoleum.

This is the home office of Biggs, Scranton & Pulver, a multi-state firm with over 250 attorneys. The firm services large corporations with deep pockets and ties to Louisville. Pathogen's home office is in Louisville and it has the deepest pocket of all of the firm's clients.

Like most big companies, they are a target for scam artists looking to make a quick buck, which is good for the firm because it keeps a large portion of the attorneys busy defending frivolous law suits. John was right about one thing, losing Pathogen's business would definitely hurt the firm. Cutbacks would follow and more than one attorney would lose his job.

There are two routes to my office. Curiosity caused me to chose the route that would take me past John's office, where I found crime scene tape barring entry. I thought about what Kruthers told me earlier and decided to have a look around to see if there was any clue as to why John killed himself. I squeezed past the yellow tape and wormed my way into his office.

Even though the place appeared to be empty, something told me to close the door behind me. Rather than turn the lights on, I used the flashlight app on my phone. I'm not sure what I expected to see, but it wasn't this.

John's office looked intact except for the obvious mess indicating a crime scene, complete with mangled chandelier and chalk outline of dead body. I thought they only did that in the movies. It sure looked like the police were treating this like a homicide rather than a suicide.

There was a stack of files on the corner of his desk that I quickly rifled through. None of them looked suspicious. There was nothing else on the desk. The desk drawers were locked. Unless I was willing to force them open, there was nothing left for me to do in this room. I just couldn't see myself breaking into John's desk.

I did one last scan of the room for anything that might shed some light on the mystery of John's death, but saw nothing out of the ordinary. I was turning to leave when I felt something under my shoe. As bent to pick up a wadded piece of paper, the doorknob turned and the office door slowly opened. Panicked, I slipped the paper into my pocket and squatted behind the desk for cover.

My mind was racing for a cover story, but I couldn't think of a plausible excuse for being in John's office. I don't know whether it's true or not, but everybody knows a criminal returns to the scene of the crime. If I was caught here, it would make me look very guilty.

I waited breathlessly for the lights to come on,

but they didn't. The only light in the room came from a full moon shining through the window. Now that my eyes had adjusted, it seemed way too bright at the moment. I risked peeking around the edge of the desk and caught a glimpse of the door just before it closed shut.

I crept over to the door and listened for a few minutes, before I decided I could risk opening it and taking a peek. The hall was empty and I slipped out. I didn't want to push my luck and thought about leaving, but I needed to do what I came for and was about to head down the hall to my office when Detective Lambers stepped in front of me.

He was gaunt. The man I remember had let himself go soft, but not this man. He was too thin and the slack skin along his jaw line made him look older than he really is. There was nothing slack about his eyes. While they were surrounded by shadow, the eyes burned with intensity. I can't be sure of their color since all I really noticed is they were bloodshot, as if he hadn't slept well recently.

He was dressed in grey slacks, a navy blue blazer that could use a trip to the dry cleaners, and a sky blue mixed cotton poly shirt that was wrinkled despite claims of being permanent press. A blue and white tie was hanging loose around an open collar that revealed a tuff of chest hair.

"Couldn't resist returning to the scene of the crime, could you?" asked Lambers.

"Geez, where did you come from?" I asked.

"Why did you kill him?" demanded Lambers.

"I didn't kill him and you know it," I said.

"I know a murderer when I see one," he said.

"You know only a deep-seated grudge and you're letting it cloud your judgment," I said.

"I have an eye witness that places you at the scene," he said.

"I work here," I said.

"Not anymore," said Lambers.

"Are you behind that?" I asked.

"I'm going to make sure you spend a lot of time in prison," he said.

"John Biggs committed suicide and if you continue to harass me, I will press charges," I said.

"Are you threatening me," he said.

"The problem with having a big mouth like yours is everybody knows your business," I said. "What that means for you is everybody knows you hate my Uncle Jim and you hate me because of him."

"Helen Gloria overheard you arguing with Biggs, just before you killed him," he said.

"We were discussing a raise when Helen interrupted us to tell John he had a call from

Zeke Kruthers," I said.

"She saw you kill him," said Lambers.

"She saw me try to save his life," I said.

"What are doing here?" he demanded.

"I came to pick up my personal belongs," I said.

"Not in Biggs' office," he said.

"Kruthers told me he delivered some bad news to John just before he killed himself, but he wouldn't tell me what it was," I said. "I was hoping to find an explanation for John's suicide"

"You violated a crime scene," said Lambers. "I should arrest your right now for obstruction of justice."

"I've never seen a man kill himself before," I said. "I needed an explanation."

"I know you killed him and I'm going to prove it," he said.

He turned and left. I shook my head and headed down the hall to my office. By no means is it a fancy corner office like John's, but it had been home to me for several years. Unlike John's office, it had been ransacked and was a total mess. One odd thing I noticed was the bottle of bourbon was gone and in its place was an empty bottle. I wondered about that, but it was time to pack and leave, except I needed a box.

I found a single box in the copy room. There was some trash in the bottom that I would have thrown away, but I couldn't find the trash can that usually sits next to the copier. I let out a sigh and carried the box, trash and all to my office with the intention of cleaning it out before I put my things in it, but when I got there the trash can from my office was gone too. I could have dumped it onto the floor, but instead, I made quick work of tossing my stuff on top of the trash and headed out.

I managed to get out of the building without further incident. Once I was on the road again, I decided I needed to stop somewhere and have a good stiff drink. It seemed like the best idea I had all day.

CHAPTER 12

My head throbbed to the beat of a rap song crackling from an old clock radio salvaged from my parents' attic. Like a scratched record, the same two annoying lines repeated again and again.

"I'm a man of Tao, naked and wild. I can make you howl, naked and wild."

Something had to be done about that throbbing. Either I needed more tequila or the radio needed to die. Since making a decision was totally out of the question, I decided to do both. First, I hit the mute button, but it didn't work. Frustrated, I stabbed it a second and then a third time. It must have been possessed, because it kept playing.

That's when a brilliant idea leaked through the alcohol haze and I yanked the cord out of the wall. The music played on. Just as I was about to take a swing at the radio, a bright light dialed the headache up to max.

I put a pillow over my face and groaned, "Just kill me now."

It didn't help. The pillow stank from last

night's sins and the radio continued tormenting me. I groaned and tossed the pillow to the floor. Then I grabbed the radio and smashed it against the wall. It couldn't have gotten much worse, but it did.

"Have you lost your mind, Grant?"

It was a chick's raspy voice, sounding like she'd smoked one too many unfiltered Camels. The voice belonged to a tall brunette with nearly two inches of dirty blond roots and chipped red nail polish. She was standing in my bathroom doorway.

There was something familiar about this woman, but I couldn't place her. She was also a little scary thanks to a tattoo of Eve holding a snake in one hand and a half-eaten apple in the other. Her face was hard-worn, as if she had seen some tough times. I thought she might look older than she actually was. I have a habit of giving strangers nicknames and tagged her Eve.

She cleared her throat expectantly, so I mumbled the first thing that came to mind, "The music woke me."

She blinked a couple of times. I wasn't sure if she was adjusting to the light, or if she was trying to decide if she should ask about the radio.

"What music?" she finally asked.

Now I was confused, so I asked a question of my own, "You didn't hear the radio?"

"No, I sure heard you though," she said. "You were dreaming…all curled up into a ball and begging someone to please stop."

The disgusted look on her face did not help with my sour stomach or pounding headache.

"It's pathetic for a grown man to act that way, if you ask me," she added.

I let out a groan. For years, my nightmares have been filled with the Fat Lady. I've tried everything I can think of to rid myself of them and failed. It was bad enough that I have to re-live that horrible experience on a nightly basis, but this judgmental behavior from the likes of her is something I won't tolerate.

I was about to ask her to leave when she shifted to another tactic.

"Do you want to pick up where we left off last night?" she asked.

I had no idea what happed last night and I hoped we didn't sleep together, but I sure wasn't going to let it happen now. Besides my head felt as if last night's tequila had taken root and a large, festering agave was growing in it. I fought back an eruption of stomach acid burning its way past my heart and half way up my esophagus, before I finally managed to choke it back down.

She was nearly to the bed when I blurted out, "I have a headache."

She froze in place and fixed a glassy stare at

the center of my forehead, as if she could see into my head.

"Really?" she asked. "You have a headache. I can't believe you just said that to me. It sounds like something I would say to my husband."

Even though it was the truth, I also hated saying it. Cynthia often used the same excuse. I heard it often enough from her that I stopped asking.

That wasn't the worst of it. Cynthia revealed her true nature on those occasions she tried to negotiate an exchange for something she wanted from me. As you can imagine, it didn't go well when I pointed out she was trying to turn a trick with her husband.

After a couple of months she told me I was emotionally bankrupt and demanded a divorce. It was just like her to make it my fault. She said she needed more from a partner than I could give. Go figure. She emptied our bank account and moved her girlfriend into the house.

Eve was looking a bit impatient as she crossed her arms over her flat chest. I didn't know what she expected me to say. I sure didn't want to talk about headaches or spouses. If anyone was due an explanation, it had to be me. Geez, she was a married woman standing in my bedroom.

I shrugged.

"The headache is real, but you have a husband at home," I said. "Maybe you should spend some time with him. I'm really not interested in married women."

"Yea, that's what you said last night," she said.

My hands were shaking. I wasn't sure if it was caused by an overdose of tequila, or the nightmarish day I had yesterday.

"I'm still not interested," I said.

Maybe I should have been more diplomatic, because it started to get ugly at this point.

"Look at you," said Eve. "You're a mess. You live above a hookah bar. I thought you were some kind of hot shot lawyer."

She was right about the apartment. It wasn't much. Two small rooms above a hookah bar in a busy section of the Highlands. The larger of the two rooms was divided by a laminated countertop into a kitchen and living room. The initials of a prior tenant were carved into the countertop and judging by the burn marks, it was once used as an ash tray.

Two mismatched thrift store bar stools lined the bar. One was solid enough, but the other was a menace. I kept meaning to throw it out before someone got hurt and sued me for what little I had. Not that I entertained guests in the place.

The half-eaten pizza and empty tequila bottle

was just the tip of the mound of trash. A stack of unopened mail lay in a pile of dust at the end of a beat up old coffee table. Several of the envelopes were marked "final notice." I should have opened the mail and paid a few bills, but I really got distracted with the big case I was working on for Goth.

The only thing of value in the place was a dusty antique sword with strange markings standing alone in the corner like a silent sentry. It was a gift from Ch'ing. With a twinkle in his eye he told me it was older than the hills, and a priceless piece of junk. I felt a stab of panic remembering that he was missing. I needed to get it together and find out what was going on.

At the end of the kitchen counter was an open door leading into a small windowless bedroom. On the floor was a king sized mattress that took up most of the room. That's where I was at the moment. The only light in the room came from a bare light bulb in the small bathroom. It provided backlighting for Eve. The truth is I would have preferred something closer to total darkness.

I sighed. I couldn't remember ever waking up with a stranger before, and didn't know how to handle it. What I did know for sure, it was time to get rid of her, but first I asked her about last night.

"For the last six months I watched you come into my bar and order the same thing," she said. "It was the most expensive bourbon in the place and never diluted with a mixer or ice."

She swept her arm around my apartment and shook her head in disbelief.

"You have that right mix of bad boy and good guy that is so delicious," she said. "There is danger lurking behind your smooth lawyer façade. I could tell you were some kind of bad ass, but I could also see a lost little boy in there too. It made you especially hot!"

"It was always the same," she continued. "You would sit at the bar and sip your one drink, while the hottest chicks in the place hit on you. Once you finished your whiskey, you would excuse yourself and go to the men's room. From there you would quietly slip out the door without saying goodbye to anyone."

"I thought you might be gay or something," she said. "What a waste that would be. I always wanted to turn a gay guy. So, last night when you started ordering shots of tequila, I saw an opportunity and decided to take it. You were interested at first, but then you noticed my ring and chilled. So, I made some adjustments."

I raised an eyebrow and asked, "Adjustments?"

"I told you my husband died in a motorcycle

wreck a few months ago and I wasn't ready to take my ring off," she answered. "You got all sappy and told me about your dad."

"But why would you lie like that," I asked.

She narrowed her eyes and said, "Because I can."

I didn't remember any of this and I didn't like her lies.

"How did we get back here?" I asked.

"Seriously…it didn't take much once you were good and drunk," answered Eve. "I let you call me Ginny and bent over every once in a while so you could peek down my shirt. We closed the deal when I followed you into the men's room. Men are so easy to manipulate."

I didn't like being manipulated and the last thing I needed was a jealous husband.

As an afterthought she asked, "Who's Ginny by the way?"

I wasn't about to discuss Ginny with this woman and decided to keep the discussion focused on her.

"Won't your husband want to know where you spent the night?" I asked.

"I'll tell him I couldn't sleep after work and went to my sister's for coffee," she said. "He's so stupid. He believes whatever I tell him."

The lies reminded me of Cynthia. I did not need another liar in my life. I was trying to figure out how to get rid of her when my phone vibrated. The call was from Eric. Getting rid of her was going to be an unpleasant task. I dislike being rude, especially to women. I don't usually take calls when I'm with someone, but it was a welcomed diversion.

"It's very early," I said.

"He lives," said Eric. "Glad you survived the night."

"What do you know about last night?" I asked.

"Only that you didn't go home after we finished searching Ch'ing's place," answered Eric. "You were seriously wasted dude and wouldn't tell me where you were. I've never seen you so paranoid. You kept jabbering some nonsense about a stalker cop, Ginny, and a kiss."

"I didn't kiss Ginny last night," I said. "You're tripping man."

"I was afraid of that," he said.

Eve was ransacking the room, all the while cursing her stupidity. I have no idea what she was looking for. The place was a mess before she started, but somehow she still managed to make it worse.

"How do you find anything in this mess?" she growled.

"I hear a chick's voice," said Eric. "Dude, you're holding out on me. Did you take Ginny home? It's about time you found someone like that. I have to say…you stayed with Cynthia way too long! What was that skanky stripper's name? You know…the one she left you for…Chasity…Candy?"

"Candida…and no I didn't bring Ginny home with me," I said.

"Unbelievable…Candida…how fitting she chose a STD for a stage name," said Eric. "It's not Ginny…bummer. Well…anyway, I'm glad you got some action last night, but if it had been me, I would have poured my energy into Ginny. That girl is special!"

Eve said a little too loudly, "You're a loser, Grant."

She slammed the door on her way out for added emphasis.

"Dude, she's really pissed," said Eric.

"Yeah, the perfect ending to a really bad night," I said wryly.

"There's nothing you can to do about the angry chick, but move forward, Grant," said Eric.

Speaking of moving forward, I asked, "Is there any news on Ch'ing?"

"No, but I've got my best guys on it," answered Eric.

"I'm worried," I said.

"Yeah, me too," said Eric.

"Stay on it," I said.

"Roger that," he said. "Oh, I almost forgot why I called. I've got a job for you."

"I don't want a job, Eric. I'm moving to Bhutan."

"Yeah right, you're broke," he said. "Let me help you out, Grant. I have a job for you."

I was suspicious.

"What kind of job?" I asked.

"Padma Ganesha needs protection," replied Eric.

"You're joking right," I said. "I'm not a bodyguard, Eric. I'm a lawyer."

"Grant, you're an unemployed lawyer," said Eric.

"How did you know they let me go?" I asked.

"Drunk talk," said Eric. "I couldn't shut you up."

"I wonder who else I called?" I said.

"Who knows," said Eric. "Anyway, Dude, you need the money and maybe it's time for a change. Besides, who knows where this could lead."

I wondered why Eric needed me to guard someone and asked, "You're the professional. Why don't you do this?"

"I would, but they asked for you," said Eric. "It's a lot of money and could keep you occupied while we get the rest of this mess sorted out."

"Asked for me...really...and who would that

be?" I asked.

"You know better than to ask that question, Grant," said Eric. "I would tell you, but then I'd have to kill you."

"Geez, you can be so incredibly corny sometimes," I said. "How about cutting the crap and telling me why the winner of the Nobel Peace prize needs a body guard?"

"Who knows, buddy," said Eric. "It'll pay a few bills and might even buy you a plane ticket to Katmandu. He is speaking today at the Center."

"I thought Padma Ganesha never did speaking engagements," I said.

"Yeah, I know," said Eric. "He surprised everyone when he accepted. The sponsor is Emerald Allure, Inc. It's part of their lecture series, Ideas to Change the World."

"Emerald Allure…isn't that Ginny's company and don't they make high-end women's clothing?" I asked.

"Sexy clothing seems like a good place to start world change to me," snickered Eric. "I find it uplifting."

I ignored Eric's sophomoric joke and searched my memory for details about Padma Ganesha. A few years ago he wrote a best-selling book about the happiest place on Earth. The inhabitants are totally at ease with themselves and the world around them. There is no hatred in their hearts. Their minds are free from worry. They live simple and honest lives, giving much and expecting little. It is a place of peace and prosperity.

It is also a place where people live long lives. The natives credit their longevity to a magical pool of water they call the "Bubbling Well".

Padma's book stayed on top of the best seller list for one hundred and thirty-six weeks. Although he never gave the place a name, the media took to calling it "Shangri La." His fans hounded him for the location of the Bubbling Well, but he steadfastly refused to reveal it.

I thought about Mom's unpaid bill and asked, "What do I have to do?"

"You should dress in black," replied Eric. "Keep it casual."

"What…no uniform boss man?" I quipped.

Eric sighed.

"Amateur," he said. "I'll send over a shirt that identifies you as security staff. Be at the Center by 6:00 p.m. Use the back stage entrance off 7th Street. Ask for Tiny at the security desk."

"Let me guess," I said. "Tiny is 6'8", weighs 350 pounds, wears a pony tail, and is covered with tattoos."

"With a face only a mother could love," said Eric. "He's a real character. This is his night job. His day job is leader of the outlaw motorcycle gang, Dragon Gate. You'll like him, Grant."

"Does Tiny have a last name?" I asked.

"If he does, I've never heard it," answered Eric.

CHAPTER 13

After ending the call with Eric, I sat on the edge of the dirty mattress and took a long hard look at myself. The apartment smelled like a toxic waste dump. I scanned the filth scattered around the room and only saw a place where chaos reigns. I had made a mess of my life.

Eve was toxic. The tequila was toxic. They were poison to me. I shook my head in the hope of ridding myself of a specter lurking in the shadows of my mind. Despair was at hand, threatening to take over.

I couldn't go on like this. It was time for change. I desperately needed to clean up and restore order to my mangled life. It was time to rid myself of the toxins, but where should I begin, I wondered.

Ch'ing likes to say that the place to begin is with a simple practice right where you are, so that's what I did. I closed my eyes, inhaled deeply and released the toxins. I repeated this simple formula over and over again with the absolute faith that it was working until peace filed my mind and there was no long any room for despair.

I sat in meditation until I knew with absolute certainty what I needed to do next. The details of a plan took shape in my mind and when it was fully fleshed out, I opened my eyes and began.

I took some niacin and washed it down with a couple of quarts of distilled water, before heading to the gym, where I found an empty aerobics room and did Tai Chi until my clothes were drenched in sweat. Then I headed to the steam room.

There was no one else taking a steam bath, so I settled down on the center of the top bench and closed my eyes. The heat washed over me in waves that melted away the last vestiges of crud. I had one thought and only one thought…restore me.

There was momentary draft of cold air and then the bench creaked next me. I heard a familiar voice.

"Well, here we are," said Goth.

He was the absolute last person I ever expected to see in the gym steam room.

"What are you doing here?" I asked.

He peered at me with dark inscrutable eyes.

"Having a steam bath, what else?" he finally answered.

"I got your message," I said.

His eyes flared hot with anger at the reminder

that I had ignored him. Then they quickly went cold again as he found a way to suppress it. He waited.

"What is it you want to discuss?" I asked.

"Nasty business, Biggs killing himself like that," he said.

I nodded.

"What do you know about it?" he asked.

"I found him hanging from the chandelier in his office, but not in time to save his life," I said.

"You spoke to him?" asked Goth.

"Yes, earlier when I told him about the verdict," I said.

"Did you discuss anything else?" he asked.

"I asked for a raise," I said.

He nodded as if he was checking items off a mental list. Many times I have seen attorneys do the same thing during depositions.

"Anything else," he said.

I shook my head.

"Did he give you any hint why he did it?" asked Goth.

"None," I answered.

"Why do you think he did it?" he asked.

Something told me not to share my conversation with Kruthers.

"I really don't know," I said.

He nodded thoughtfully.

"It's unfortunate that the firm let you go," he

said.

"I didn't deserve it," I said.

His eyes got that predatory look I had seen before.

"Not to worry," he said. "There may be something for you to do for me. I'll be in touch."

He then abruptly got up and left the steam room without another word.

Once I had enough heat, I took a cold shower before heading over to Shady Days to see Mom. There was something important I needed to tell her.

Ginger waved me over as soon as I stepped into the building. Without a word, she walked around her desk and gave me a warm hug.

"How is she?" I asked.

She shook her head.

"Ms. Li still isn't awake," she said. "Let's assume the best. We heal ourselves, and to do it right, we need plenty of rest."

"You're right about the rest," I said. "I won't stay too long."

"She's strong," said Ginger.

I nodded.

"Is she still in ICU?" I asked.

She shook her head.

"The Doctor moved her back to her room," said Ginger.

"Would you tell the Doctor I want an update on her condition?" I asked.

Ginger had been less than her usual chatty self and more focused than usual. I guess it was a bit too much to ask for, because she suddenly resumed her usual behavior.

"Oh, you know how those Doctors are, Grant," said Ginger. "Getting one to think about anything other than their next big purchase isn't easy. Why Dr. Michaels was just saying that he is looking at vacation homes in Bermuda. Like you really have to own a home just to visit a place."

She shook her head and continued mumbling to herself as I headed off to Mom's room.

The door was open and noise from a television rerun could be heard inside. Part of Mom's therapy is to leave it on for several hours a day to keep her mind stimulated. The curtains were open wide and the midday light was flooding in. I turned the television off and sat in the rocker next to her bed.

Her eyes were closed, but I could see her chest rising and falling with each breath. Her hair was pulled back, making her already gaunt face look just a little thinner. I took her boney hand in mine and held it as I rocked the chair ever so slightly.

I'm not sure how long we sat like that, maybe an hour or so, before I was able to tell her that I needed to sell her house to pay the nursing home bill. I didn't know if she could hear me or not, but I wanted to tell her in person. Her home was the last place she had known happiness…it was the last place I had known happiness. It was time to move on with our lives.

I gave her hand another squeeze, promised I would soon return and then left. That was the hard part. Now I needed to swing by the house and tell Cynthia it's time for her to leave.

There was a Subaru Outback in the driveway behind my Benz, so I parked on the street. I figured it belonged to her lover. When she didn't answer the third knock I dug into my pocket for the house key, but before I could use it, the door jerked open.

"What are you doing here, Grant?" demanded Cynthia.

"You need to gather your things and leave," I said.

I could see from the look on her face that my answer surprised her, but it didn't take her long to regroup and return to her usual bully self.

"I filed for a divorce or haven't you heard yet?" she asked.

"The sheriff delivered your message," I said.

"Good, then you know that I've asked for the house," she said.

"This house doesn't belong to you," I said.

"We'll see about that, my attorney says…"

I interrupted her.

"I'm selling the house," I said. "I'll be listing it with a realtor when I leave here."

"You can't just do that," said Cynthia.

"Really, when did you get a law degree, Cynthia," I said.

"The judge will decide who gets this house," she said.

"No he won't," I said.

"I'm calling the police," she said.

I waited.

"I'm calling them now," she said and pulled her phone from a pocket.

"Go ahead," I said. "They will tell you to call your attorney and then leave."

She hesitated.

"I'm calling my attorney," she said.

"Go ahead," I said.

This time she actually hit the call button. I waited.

"This is Cynthia Li," she said. "Let me speak to Ms. Kingsport."

"If you are lucky enough to get through to her, tell her the house is deeded jointly to my parents," I said. "This is Mom's house and you are trespassing."

Cynthia's eyes opened wide in disbelief. There was a certain amount of satisfaction seeing her go slack jaw with shock. Without another word, I turned and left.

What happened next wasn't part of the plan. Ginny grew up around the corner from me. Not once after the incident with her mother did I venture down their street. Her mother still lives around the corner from Mom's house, and as I walked away from Cynthia, I surprised even myself when I turned toward Ginny's old house.

I stood on the sidewalk and stared at it for the longest time. Overgrown shrubs blocked much of the narrow sidewalk and obscured the front of the house. There were no lights on or signs of life inside.

It was a hot muggy day and all the other homes along the street were buttoned up tight with air conditioners running full blast. Her house was the only exception. The front door was open, allowing fresh air to flow into the house through an ornamental security door with no glass, just a screen for bugs.

Using the butterflies in my stomach to galvanize myself, I walked up the front steps and onto a small porch. I paused for a moment and considered turning back. My hand reached for the door of its own accord and knocked.

"In the kitchen," called out her mother in a heavily accented voice. "I'm baking and my hands are full. Come on in."

I'm not sure what I expected, but it wasn't that. I took a deep breath and stepped over the threshold.

The inside looked like a mother's house. It was neat and orderly. Scattered around the living room were photographs taken at various stages of life. A scrap quilt patterned as a crucifix was draped over the back of the sofa. The agony of Jesus was the focal point. Facing the corner sat a straight backed chair made from dark hardwood. An open Bible rested in the seat. The house was filled with a familiar aroma.

The kitchen was around the corner to the right. The oven door was standing open. A plump middle aged Spanish woman with a loose strand of graying hair draped over the right side of her face was turning toward the counter top with a sheet of cookies. My knees weakened.

"I made your favorite...hot almond cookies," she said. "Don't they smell delicious? Would you..."

Her chattering stopped abruptly and the smile evaporated. She narrowed her eyes and glared at me over the top of her glasses.

"You...you...you're that abomination...the bastard son of mixed parents," she stuttered. "What are you doing in my house?"

"I knocked," I said. "You invited me in."

Maria tilted her head slightly, planted her fists

onto her ample hips and glared at me.

"I thought it was my daughter coming to visit," she said.

"I have something I want to tell you," I said.

Maria barked, "I don't care what you have to tell me. Get out of my house you nasty little boy...out!"

"I'm not a little boy anymore and I'm not afraid of you," I said. "You're a hateful woman and from this day forward I will gladly leave you behind to wallow in your own misery."

The last thing I heard as I stepped out the door was her prayer, "Hail Mary, full of grace..."

CHAPTER 14

The Center is located in downtown Louisville on the Ohio River at water's edge. While not far from the apartment, it was too far to walk on a hot day, so I headed out in dad's old truck. Traffic was bumper to bumper on Main Street. Horns were honking. People were partying in the streets. Their hands were stuffed with super sized beers and foot long hot dogs.

Street vendors were selling t-shirts that read, "Immortality Is Only Kinky the First Time." It was a festive carnival atmosphere. I wondered if these people really believed they were going to learn the secret of immortality, or if it was just another reason to get rowdy.

Even though the event didn't begin until 7:00 p.m., the Center parking garage was already jammed packed when I arrived a few minutes before six. I made my way to the rooftop where I spotted one last empty space at the end of a row.

Before I could park, a green Porsche whipped around the corner heading in the wrong direction and straight at me. A brunette with wavy hair blowing in the wind was behind the wheel. A phone was stuck in her ear. She was focused on her conversation and did not see me.

I hit the brakes hard enough that I was jerked forward and smashed into the steering wheel. A sharp pain shot through my sternum as the Porsche slipped into the last spot.

The chick was completely oblivious. I leaned out of the window intending to give her a hard time about what she'd just done, but stopped short when I heard her shouting into the phone.

"I'm sorry you feel that way," she said.

When she turned and dropped the phone into her purse I got a good look at her face for the first time. It was Ginny. She opened the door and gracefully swung her legs out of the Porsche. I forgot the pain in my sternum. I forgot she stole my parking space. I forgot she nearly crashed into me. Damn, if I didn't forget to breathe.

Then to my utter amazement her grace evaporated into a spell of clumsiness as she awkwardly dropped her car keys onto the pavement. When she bent over to pick them up I heard the unmistakable sound of tearing fabric.

"You've got to be kidding me!" she said.

Still oblivious to my presence she tried looking over her shoulder for the torn fabric. When that didn't work she twisted at the waist. Finally, she bent over and tried to peer up her dress.

When she looked up for the first time, she saw me watching her from the truck. Her jaw dropped as we made eye contact and I smiled.

"Your dress is torn," I said.

Her beautiful eyes narrowed slightly. I tried again.

"You need some help with it?" I asked.

She mumbled something I couldn't make out. Turning on a heel she stomped off in the direction of the stairwell. For the first time, I could see the rip down the small of her back revealing a glimpse of her tattoo.

"A Porsche," I muttered. "I'm sure she was real impressed with my truck."

Since Ginny had taken the last available parking space, I reluctantly parked the pickup in front of a no parking sign at the end of the row. There was a good chance it would be impounded. At that point, I just didn't care.

It was the first time I had ever been back stage. I expected security to be tight at all of the entrances, but there was literally no one attending the door. I quietly surveyed my surroundings. To the right was a small vending area with several empty tables. To the left was a security office. Straight ahead was a corridor with a sign posted at the entrance that read, "Authorized Personnel Only." I didn't see Tiny anywhere.

I returned my attention to the security office. The overhead light was on, but the view into the room was obscured by a smoked glass window. I could barely make out the outline of a desk surrounded by security monitors. No one was sitting in the desk chair. The office looked empty to me. I figured Tiny was making his rounds, but since the door to the office stood wide open I decided to just have a peek inside.

As I moved closer to the office door I smelled it for the second time in the last twenty-four hours…a strange combination of coffee, rust, and shit. I froze in place, listening for any sound that would explain the now familiar odors. The last few drops of a fresh pot gurgled from a coffee maker. I heard nothing else, so I peeked cautiously inside the door.

A mountain of a man, obviously Tiny, was lying in a pool of blood. His meaty hands were grasping at the hilt of a combat knife that had been buried in his chest. I rushed to his side and dropped to my knees. Tiny's head rolled in my direction. His pupils were large and unfocused. Blood trickled from the side of his mouth. He tried to speak, stopped, and then gurgled something that sounded like "Mung."

I wiped his mouth with my shirt tail and laid my hands on top his to stop him from pulling the knife out.

"Don't," I said. "Just hang on. I'll get help."

I dug into my pocket and pulled out my phone. It squirted from my blood soaked hand and landed on the floor a few feet away. A thin stream of blood squirted from the edge of the wound.

"Damn," I cursed.

I needed both hands to stop the loss of blood. Tiny needed medical attention fast. How was I going to get help? I had to make that call. Tiny's life depended on it. Trying to keep pressure on the wound with one hand, I stretched the other hand toward the phone. Just as my fingertips reached it, a foot came out of nowhere and kicked it across the room. The phone bounced off a metal file cabinet and spun out of reach on the other side of Tiny.

In the corner my eye, I saw a sandaled heel pivot and point in my direction. I instinctively rolled under a back kick that would have crushed my chest and slammed hard into the attacker's supporting leg. The maneuver worked. His knee gave way and he crumbled to the ground.

I thought I had him, but quick as a cat, he popped to his feet. I lurched at him with blood soaked hands, but missed. The miss cost me dearly. I never saw the foot that slammed into my ribs or the hand that grabbed my throat a second later. Before I could retaliate, his knee pinned my arm to the floor. This guy was fast.

Instinct is to pull away, but Ch'ing had trained me well. Instead of trying to yank my arm away from him, I rolled in the direction of the pinned arm and slammed a palm into the back of his elbow. It worked. He grunted in pain and released my throat as he tried to tumble away from me.

I followed close behind, but he caught his balance and I caught his fist in my sore ribs. Grimacing in pain, my hand clutched at a cracked rib. It was instinctive, but the wrong move because it gave him a chance to roll to his feet and flee the room.

I wanted to follow him, but scrambled back to Tiny instead. His pupils were fully dilated. The bleeding had stopped. I checked his pulse. It confirmed what I already knew. Tiny was dead. My second death in two days. What was happening? People around me were dropping like flies.

There was nothing I could do for Tiny, but I could do something about his killer. Determined to catch him, I pulled the knife from Tiny's chest and scrambled after the killer. I didn't make it far before I slipped on the blood soaked floor and crashed head first into the door jam. The blow brought me to my knees, stars dancing before my eyes, and then I blacked out.

I'm not sure how long I was out. When I came to I remember gingerly touching my brow and feeling something wet. I looked at my finger tips and saw blood. I vaguely remember thinking I needed a doctor. I stuck a hand into my pocket to call one, but couldn't find the phone.

I was disoriented. It was the sight of Tiny's body that brought it all back. I pulled myself together as best I could, grabbed my phone and the knife before staggering out of the office. I headed for the door marked "Authorized Personnel Only" which opened into a long corridor. I was pretty sure it was the direction the killer took thanks to the blood stains on the floor, but the trail he left didn't last for long.

The passageway was lined with doors. As I rushed down the hallway, I looked for something that would tell me which way the killer might have headed. There were more doors on the left, the N.E. Stairs, and an elevator. The elevator did not appear to be moving.

I peeked into the stairwell, but didn't hear any footsteps. I was about to turn back when a small bit of blood dripped at my feet. Another drop followed, but this one splattered on my wrist. I looked upward and caught a glimpse of crimson fabric. The monk was on the landing above me, waiting for my next move.

Rather than rush in and try to chase him

down, I decided on stealth. Ch'ing taught me that the secret to moving with stealth is balance. The key to balanced movement is to never move a weighted foot. You must take all the weight off a foot before you move it.

As quietly as I could, I stepped into the stairwell and let the door close behind me. Still as a tree, I waited to see what the monk did next. He didn't budge, so I inched toward the first step as quietly as I could. I stopped and waited again. Everything looked good, so I started up the stairs. One by one, I slowly climbed the steps. All the while, my neck stretched to catch a peek of the monk before he saw me.

Laying in a crumpled mess on the landing was the monk's discarded robe. It was damp with fresh blood. Disappointment washed over me. I nudged the robe with a toe and saw a slice in it. Tiny must have gotten in some blows and gone down fighting.

I didn't get a good look at the killer's face. Without the robe to distinguish him from everyone else, I had little hope of finding him. He could be anyone. There were over three thousand people at the Center to hear Padma reveal his big secret. Finding the killer in that crowd was definitely beyond my skill level.

Besides, I didn't know whether he used the stairwell to dump his disguise, or if he took the stairs to a different floor. The Center is a big place and Tiny's murderer could be anywhere. Capturing Tiny's killer would have to be left to the police. It was time to call them, but first I wanted to wash the blood from my hands.

I didn't have any trouble finding a bathroom, but I was preoccupied and didn't pay much attention to the sign on the door. I wish I had. Instead, I rushed in, set the knife next to the sink and began cleaning up.

As the blood swirled down the drain, I thought about the statement I would give to the police. That is when it hit me. I had made another huge mistake. I was in the ladies room. It is also the exact moment the door opened and Ginny walked in.

She took one look at me and froze before the door closed behind her. At first there was an odd confused look on her face, but then it changed to concern.

"Oh my god, Grant, is that blood?" she asked.

I don't know what I expected from her, but after last night I knew she was a player. More to the point, despite what Kinsey said about her, I figured she didn't care one way or the other about me. I wasn't sure what to think about her concerned behavior.

"I was just cleaning up," I answered. "I guess I missed some."

She fumbled in the purse hanging on her shoulder and said, "Let's get you a doctor."

"I'm okay," I said. "It's not my blood."

Her concern shifted to confusion and then to shock.

"What do you mean it's not your blood?" she asked.

I didn't like the direction this was headed and said, "It belongs to someone else."

I was about to explain what happened when she noticed the knife. She started to say something and then snapped her mouth shut. It was her eyes that instantly concerned me the most. They were filled with terror. I had seen the same look in the eyes of witnesses I badgered during cross-examination. I hated it.

Ginny took a cautious step back. When I extended a hand in her direction, her eyes widened in alarm and then she fled the room.

"Not good," I muttered.

I'm ashamed to say, I considered fleeing. I wish I could say I decided to do the right thing instead of running, but the truth is I wanted to protect myself. I knew if she called the police and told them about the bloody knife, they would lock me in the deepest hole they had. Therefore, I went after her. It wasn't until much later that I realized I had forgotten the murder weapon.

Once out of the bathroom, I scanned the hall

for her. She was nowhere in sight. I couldn't understand how she managed to disappear so quickly. She could be anywhere. I took a moment to weigh my options, but what I did instead was feel sorry for myself. I had done nothing wrong, but everything that could possibly go wrong, had gone wrong. First John and now this! What else could go wrong, I thought. The answer is plenty and it did.

When I regained my composure, I noticed an unmarked door standing open. I was pretty sure it was closed earlier and decided to take a look inside. There were several rows of alternating stage lights hanging from the ceiling separated by sliding curtains and open moveable wall partitions. A simple podium was the only stage prop. I could hear the buzz of the audience's conversation. Somehow I had managed to find the stage.

That's when I remembered I was there to protect Padma. I had a job to do and that was what I needed to take my mind off myself.

I didn't have a clue what to do next. There was one thing I knew for sure...I had no training as a body guard and there was a killer on the loose. Ch'ing would tell me to listen, not just with my ears, but with my whole being. Sighing, I wondered what that meant and decided the only thing to do was wait and see what happened next.

I chose a position out of the way, but with a strategic view of the podium and audience. The audience was an odd crowd…a cross section of America. For example, a hippie chick in the front row sat next to man in a conservative business suit. The rest of the crowd was equally incongruent.

Leaning lightly against the wall, I felt something poke me in the back and looked over my shoulder. It was a bank of light switches for the stage lights.

When I turned around again, the guy Ginny left the party with last night was on the opposite side of the stage watching me! What was Pony Tail he doing here and why did he have a gun tucked into his jeans?

CHAPTER 15

The audience erupted into applause as Ginny walked across the stage. Her step had lost its spring and her eyes were noticeably puffy. At first it puzzled me to see her on stage, but then I remembered she was the CEO of the program sponsor, Emerald Allure, Inc. Despite the bombshell good looks and the hot clothes, Ginny feels like the girl-next-door. It's easy to forget she is a rich and powerful woman...the kind of person who can summon the police. I figured she had them searching the premises for me now.

At least I would have help finding Tiny's killer. I turned my attention to Pony Tail. He was at Eric's party and now here. To make matters worse, he might be the master of disguise, so I couldn't be certain where else he would show up. The best way to be invisible is to appear ordinary. While Tibetan monks aren't a common sight in Louisville, that disguise was a stroke of genius today. Tiny must have thought he was with Padma.

If Tiny had read Padma's book, then he would have known that Buddhists believe all life is precious. They won't even dig a hole without carefully sifting the earthworms from the soil and moving them to safety. Tiny would not have felt threatened by a Tibetan monk. I figured he never saw it coming.

If Pony Tail was the killer, he must have changed into the hippie clothes after he ditched the robe. It was a perfect disguise to blend in with this peace and love crowd. Still, I couldn't be certain he wasn't another body guard like me hired to protect Padma. I decided to keep a close eye on him.

The gun concerned me, but he made no move for it. Instead his eyes were locked onto Ginny. The way he watched her every move bothered me. What were they talking about last night at Eric's party and what is he doing here?

Ginny stood before the packed house. She was focused on the audience and did not acknowledge me or Pony Tail. Given her reaction to the bloody knife a few minutes earlier, I wasn't sure what to expect from her. Was she going to cancel the event while the police searched for the murderer...searched for me? The buzz from the audience slowly subsided until you could have heard a pin drop in the place. Everyone waited, including me.

Slowly Ginny began to smile. It seemed to radiate from her whole being. I was certain you could feel the smile in her touch and when she began to speak, you could hear it in her voice. This is not what I expected at all!

"Hello. My name is Virginia Bardough, but my friends call me Ginny. So, please call me Ginny. I want to thank you for joining us at this session of Ideas to Change the World. These presentations are offered to you on faith. Not blind faith, but absolute faith in you."

"We hold the sincere belief that each of you has everything you need to have an impact on the world," she said. "Sometimes all it takes to get things going is a little reminder of what could be. So without further fanfare, we would like to present a remarkable man who inspires us with his simple message."

Ginny paused for dramatic effect before saying, "We are sovereign."

Her shining eyes surveyed the audience. One by one she pointed to individuals in the audience and repeated, "You are sovereign."

The audience was riveted to their seats by the spell she had cast.

She scanned the crowd before adding, "No one has the right to interfere with a sovereign's decisions. You decide how to live your life."

Ginny owned the audience.

"Now that I have your attention, ladies and gentlemen, please give Padma Ganesha a warm welcome," she said.

The crowd erupted into cheers and applause as a small round man in Tibetan Buddhist's crimson robes waddled onto the stage. His tiny hands were held high above his head with the palms facing the audience. He took a few steps and stopped. A smile stretched across his round boyish face. Bowing he brought his hands to his heart. The audience went wild. The little guy was like a rock star.

Padma repeatedly bowed to the audience. After five minutes of standing ovation, he finally moved prayer hands to his left shoulder and tilted his head to the side as if saying, "Give it a rest folks." The crowd roared with laughter at his good natured gesture and began to quiet down.

He took a step toward the podium, paused as if he had seen it for the first time, and then a sly grin tweaked the corners of his mouth. Taking the last few steps in its direction, he slipped behind the podium and disappeared. Well sort of. He was much wider than the podium, but the top of his head was barely visible.

If it wasn't for the extra three inches the green cowboy boots gave him, he may not have made it to the top. Seriously…green cowboy boots! The combination of red and green made him look like a chubby little Christmas elf.

An awkward silence descended over the

audience before it was broken by a lady in the front row who said, "You'd think somebody would have thought of this."

As if on cue, Padma peeked around the side of the podium like a child playing a game of peek-a-boo. A few in the audience laughed nervously. Most were quiet.

The ensuing silence was broken by an outrageously long and noisy fart. Padma let out a sigh of relief. The audience shifted uncomfortably in their seats.

You could have heard a pin drop before an old man in the front row busted out with laughter. Padma turned to me and winked through thick black rimmed glasses. As I stood there in shock, he stepped away from the podium and began speaking in a singsong voice.

"Hello again dear friends," he said. "Are you ready to learn the secret of a long life?"

Mr. Giggles in the front row said, "Damn right I am."

The crowd applauded.

Padma pointed to Mr. Giggles.

"If you could live forever, what would you do differently?" asked Padma.

Mr. Giggles didn't hesitate.

"I'd live life without regret," he answered.

"What is it you regret my friend," asked Padma.

"I did what I was told instead of doing what I wanted," answered Mr. Giggles.

Padma leaned toward Mr. Giggles and in a conspiratorial tone asked, "Do you want to hear a secret?"

Thirty two hundred hungry souls eagerly leaned forward in their seats. They came from all over the world to learn the secret of happiness and long life.

Padma gave them a relaxed peaceful smile and said, "The secret is…"

I felt a sudden chill. Pony Tail reached for his gun. Without thinking, I hit the light switches and bolted toward the podium.

"Gun, everybody down!" I shouted.

The handgun exploded. I ignored the ringing in my ears and tried to adjust my eyes to the sudden change in lighting. I suddenly felt Pony Tail to my right and turned him so that I had his back. Knowing I needed to disarm him quickly, I hooked his throat with my left hand and tilted his head until his back was bent like a bow.

Once his balance was broken, I owned him. I slid my right hand down his shooting arm. Something was wrong. There was no gun and the arm was soft. It was definitely not Pony Tail's arm.

The stage area filled with the smell of gunpowder and fear. Still, I caught a whiff of a vaguely familiar scent and buried a nose in my captive's hair. It was not a man's smell. Nor was it perfumed. It was natural and real. This had to be Ginny. I decided to hold on to her.

A second shot was fired. The first shot must have shocked the audience. The second woke them from their stunned silence. Shrill screams and fearful shouts of escape filled the hall.

My first instinct was to get Ginny to safety. Thinking of Padma, I resisted the temptation to rush to an exit. It was also my job to protect him.

As my eyes slowly adjusted to the limited light cast from the emergency exits, I scanned the area for Padma. He wasn't on the stage. Where could he be? Beyond the stage, I saw shadowy shapes moving toward the auditorium exits. The shooter seemed to have disappeared into the shadows. Ginny was tense, taking shallow breaths, but she didn't try to get away from me.

People were stampeding the exits. It was starting to get ugly. The mood of the peace and love crowd had changed dramatically. Panic was growing and the shrieking intensified as people fought their way to safety.

I whispered to Ginny, "We need to get out of here before the gunman finds us in the dark. Come with me. Try to move quietly."

She didn't budge. Since I couldn't see her

expression in the dark, I wondered if she heard me over the screams. Maybe she panicked. Finally, her head nodded slightly. Good, I thought, she's calm. I took her firmly by the elbow and we maneuvered through the stage curtains. An exit sign above the double doors glowed in the dark. We headed toward it.

Just as we reached the door, I heard footsteps behind us. Without looking back, we hurried out the door and took the stairs to the parking garage. The door opened behind us and someone followed us down the stairs.

We burst into the parking garage and rushed to the concrete steps leading to the rooftop. There were four flights to climb before we reached the top level. My breathing was ragged and the broken ribs were killing me. Ginny showed no signs of exhaustion.

We sprinted toward the truck. Ginny quickly surveyed the rust bucket before allowing herself a small smile.

"Maybe we should take my car," she said.

I turned to the Porsche and my pulse quickened. Damn, I wanted to drive that car more than anything and despite the situation, could hardly contain my excitement. I nodded in agreement.

At that instant, the stairwell door burst open and clanged against the wall. I immediately turned toward it and dropped to a crouch. There was a flash of crimson and for a moment I thought it was the killer before I finally recognized Padma's smiling face.

He headed toward us at a turtle's pace. I'd forgotten all about my charge...some bodyguard I turned out to be.

"Are you injured?" I asked.

Padma's gaze dropped to my ribs before answering with a smile, "No."

I followed his eyes. There was fresh blood on my shirt mixed in with Tiny's dried blood. I was about to explain the blood when Ginny took a step back.

"Oh my god Grant, you've been shot!" she said.

CHAPTER 16

Great! On top of everything else, now I've been shot. I could walk away right now and be done with it. All I have to do is climb into the truck and head back to that dump I call home. It may not be much, but it provides a safe haven where I can pick up the pieces of my shattered life while this broken body heals itself.

Yet, I knew I was already in too deep, and whatever this was, I would have to see it through to the end. Besides, I'd never be able to look Ch'ing in the eye again if I quit…assuming we find him.

I took a mental step back to evaluate this growing catastrophe. John is dead and a cop with a score to settle with my family is trying to pin it on me. Someone dressed as a monk stabbed Tiny to death and then broke my ribs, but since I was careless enough to leave the murder weapon in the Ladies room covered in Tiny's blood and my fingerprints, Detective Lambers will think I killed him. He's going to love that.

That loud sigh I heard was coming from me. I

had messed up big time. Instead of chasing after Tiny's killer, I should have called the police and reported the murder. I didn't do the right thing because I wasn't ready to face another barrage of questions from Detective Lambers.

Tiny's murder would only increase scrutiny of the circumstances surrounding John's death. I needed evidence proving John had a motive to kill himself, but my only lead comes from a spooked prosecutor who is keeping what he knows close to his chest. Now I would have to prove my innocence in two deaths....so much for innocent until proven guilty.

On top of everything, I was completely confused by Ginny. She magically reappears in my life and then I see her flirting with a man who has since wounded me while trying to kill Padma. Ginny disappeared from the party without a saying a word to anyone, but when I next saw her in the parking lot, she totally blew me off. Afterwards, she flipped-out when she saw me with a bloody knife...as if I was a psycho killer or something.

I could feel Padma waiting for a decision and searched his face for answers. The only thing I saw in his eyes was infinite compassion. They contained no boundaries, no limits, and it felt as if I was pulled me into a bottomless well.

I shook my head and willed myself back to the

present. Here I stand in a parking garage with a monk, who I'm supposed to protect because I got fired from my real job. It should have been an easy task, but no, a gun-toting hippie wants to kill him. I couldn't imagine why anyone would want to kill such a gentle man, but there was one thing I knew for sure, there was a killer on the loose and whatever was going on could probably get me killed too.

The killer was still out there somewhere and needed to be apprehended before he hurt someone else. Or worse, tracked us down and hurt one of us. Every second was critical and I didn't hear any police sirens rushing to our aid. Where were the cops?

One of my favorite law school professors, Laurence Filmore, once told a room full of first year law students that the police have no duty to protect us. We were discussing a wrongful death case filed by the parents of a teenage girl who was brutally raped and murdered after the police failed to respond to a 9-1-1 emergency call. The Supreme Court ruled in favor of the police and threw out the grieving family's lawsuit. They said it was law enforcement's job to investigate crime and apprehend criminals, not protect individual citizens.

I knew we were on our own. It was my job to protect Padma, and I would get no help from the police. Still, Pony Tail was on the loose and it was their job to apprehend him. It was unlikely this ordeal would be over anytime soon. While I wasn't feeling very optimistic about it, I hoped we could work together on this. It was time to call the cops even though they would have plenty of hard questions for me.

My phone was grimy with dried blood and didn't open when I swiped a finger across the screen. Resisting the temptation to fling it across the garage, I wiped it on the front of my shirt, but that only made it worse.

"Should I call an ambulance?" asked Ginny.

She was staring at a bullet hole in my shirt. I was pretty sure it was just a scratch, so I shook my head.

"No, did you call the police earlier?" I asked.

Ginny held my gaze. Her eyes were clear and calm. I could feel her searching for confirmation that she made the right choice. After a long moment, she shook her head.

"No, I didn't," she answered. "What do you think we should do?"

"Do you trust me?" I asked.

She gave me another long appraising look before answering, "Yes."

I felt relieved. It was less likely she would call the police if she trusted me. Trust is a critical component in a relationship. Without it, there isn't much chance for it.

"Then let's call the police," I said.

Ginny nodded and reached into her purse, but before she could locate her phone, we were startled by the sound of screaming tires and she spilled the purse onto the garage floor. Someone was speeding up the ramp and headed in our direction. Given the shooting, people should be in a hurry to get out of the garage. This guy was racing to the rooftop. Nothing good was going to come of this.

"We need to get out of here," I shouted.

Ginny had squatted down to gather up her things. I looked at the two seats in the Porsche and sighed. Trying to hide my disappointment, I grabbed Ginny's arm and pulled her up.

I did my best to build a sense of urgency into Padma, but the man moved like a turtle. I had a feeling if he didn't get a move on, we would live to regret it. Maybe everything was starting to get to me, but that's no excuse for the rising irritation I felt.

I was about to bark at Padma when he winked at me and said, "The way of long life is slow and easy."

I blinked. That sounded exactly like something Ch'ing would say. Padma held my gaze with calm eyes. It felt to me like he reached into the center of my being and stilled my soul.

Only Ch'ing has ever been able to do that. It occurred to me that Padma may know something about Ch'ing's whereabouts, but that would have to wait for later.

Once I got Ginny and Padma to the truck, the mercurial little guy shifted gears and now sounded like a twelve year old as he clapped his hands and called out in his high pitched voice, "Shotgun! Shotgun! I call shotgun!"

Padma slipped in front of Ginny as she reached for the door handle, climbed into the truck, and closed the door in her face. The little turtle can move when he wants to. Instead of being upset by Padma's rude behavior, Ginny's shoulders were shaking with barely contained laughter. I was instantly caught off guard by her unexpected sense of humor. I helped Ginny climb into the truck from the driver's side and slipped in next to her feeling a lot better about her.

She smelled delicious, like fresh baked bread. To take my mind off her yummy smell, I took one last look at the Porsche before starting the truck and shifting into reverse. We were nearly out when a black SUV roared around the corner and sped toward us. This maniac wanted to smash us into the concrete wall!

I slammed it into first gear and gunned the truck back into the parking spot. The SUV clipped the corner of the truck and went spinning into the Porsche. The crash echoed through the garage like thunder.

Ginny's beautiful car was a crumbled wreck. A billowing cloud of smoke drifted in our direction. I couldn't see the driver through the tinted windows, but suspected it might be Pony Tail. I had all I was going to take from this creep.

"Wait here," I said.

As I opened the door to investigate, the SUV's driver side window lowered and a gun barrel peeped out.

"Duck," I screamed.

The garage exploded in gunfire. Shattered glass sprayed across the back of my neck. I backed the truck out without looking and then gunned the engine down the ramp. We raced out of the garage and turned right on 7th Street. It was a block to River Road, where we made a right. I accelerated past the YUM Center and headed east toward Prospect. I kept checking the rearview mirror for the SUV and didn't see any sign of it. I sped out of town along River Road. I needed to get somewhere safe where I could lay low and think.

"Where are we going?" asked Ginny.

"We need to lose the SUV," I answered. "I'm headed to my Uncle's house. He will know what to do next."

The truck has a standard transmission mounted on the floor. Ginny's left thigh was squeezed next to the shifter. Each time I changed gears my wrist brushed her leg. It triggered thoughts of tearing fabric in the parking lot. I glanced down. The short dress was hiked up and revealed damn near all of her legs.

I willed my eyes up. They came to rest on her cleavage, which didn't help much with the distraction problem, so I locked my eyes forward on the road ahead.

Thinking it would help to shift my focus, I opened my mouth to ask Padma why someone wanted him dead, but nothing came out. My throat was dry. I tried to swallow, but nothing happened. As I struggled to find my voice, Ginny turned toward Padma. She studied him closely before asking the question for me.

In response, he laughed and jiggled like a department store Santa. Ginny looked at him like he'd lost his mind. The laughter finally stopped. The jiggling took a bit longer. She waited patiently.

Finally, he said, "What makes you think someone wants to kill me?"

"You were about to reveal a big secret just before someone fired two shots at you," she answered. "They want you dead for some reason."

Padma ripped off a long noisy fart and said, "Life and death are two sides of the same coin."

Ginny opened her mouth and then closed it again. To our utter amazement, Padma began singing a popular teenybopper hit. A silly little song popularized by a half-naked pre-pubescent girl. It was something about lost innocence.

An incoming call interrupted his song. I tried to dig the phone out of my jeans pocket without straightening my legs, but the pants were too tight. Cursing under my breath, I stretched and finally managed to get hold of it, but by the time I got it out of my pocket, the ringing had stopped. The missed call was from Eric.

I considered waiting until we arrived at Uncle Jim's place to return Eric's call, but the phone went off again. I figured it must be important and answered it.

"There's trouble dude," said Eric.

"The last twenty four hours have been nothing but trouble," I replied.

"Are you sitting down because it just got worse?" asked Eric.

"What is it now?"

"I just got a call from a friend with LMPD," answered Eric. "They are under pressure to bring you in, Grant. You've made some powerful enemies."

"It will have to wait," I said. "Any news on Ch'ing?"

"Not a thing," answered Eric.

"Stay at it," I said. "In the meantime, I'm headed to Uncle Jim's."

"Good idea," said Eric. "Maybe he can call in a few favors from his friends on the force. Wait a minute, Grant. Something just occurred to me, the lecture can't be over yet. What's going on?"

"Too much to tell you over the phone," I answered. "Ginny and Padma are with me."

Eric groaned.

"I got a feeling I'm not going to like this," he said.

"There was another murder," I said.

There was a long pause before Eric finally said, "Geez, another one! What happened?"

"It was Tiny," I answered. "I'm sorry, Eric. I'll fill you in on the details later."

"Damn...I got him that job," said Eric. "There's some crazy shit going down. Do you think there is a connection to John's death?"

"It would have seemed like a stretch before, but now I don't know what to think about all of this," I answered.

"You can't put the cops off much longer," said Eric. "If you delay too long, it will look like you've got something to hide."

He was right, of course. I couldn't put them

off much longer. Sooner or later, they would find me and if they did, it was unlikely my word would be enough. The pressure was on to find proof of my innocence for two deaths, and I needed it fast.

If I learned anything as a trial lawyer, I learned that you never know where the answers to a problem might turn up. I remembered something that was bugging me about this job.

"Eric, you said this morning they wanted me to guard Padma," I said. "Who are they?"

"I don't know," answered Eric. "Someone else took the call. I thought it was odd myself. I'll have one of my people look into it. Have you asked Padma?"

I hate it when I miss the obvious.

"Good idea," I said sheepishly.

After I ended the call with Eric, I intended to ask Padma about the security job, but happened to glance in the rear view mirror. There was a black SUV coming up fast!

CHAPTER 17

I hoped it wasn't the same SUV that tried to run us over in the parking garage, but of course the passenger side head lamp was smashed in and there were streaks of green paint on its front bumper. I just wished I knew who I was dealing with. There were a lot of unanswered questions, but right now I needed to do something about the SUV.

There were several options. I could try to lose them in traffic, but River Road doesn't have much traffic to speak of, unless you include the occasional biker enjoying his favorite scenic byway. I didn't think the old truck would outrun the SUV, so that was out.

In the movies, they run traffic lights or make last minute turns, but neither would work here since there are very few traffic signals and a last minute turn would most likely end up in the river. Trying to lose them just wasn't a good option.

We could stop and confront them, but the last time I tried to do that they shot at me. I did have a .357 magnum under the seat of the truck, but a wild-west shoot out in a residential area did not seem like the best option. The last encounter we had with them was in an isolated area of a parking garage. It's possible they would be less likely to shoot at us on a public road, but I didn't want to risk it. There were homes along this street and I didn't want an innocent bystander to get hurt.

We could set a trap. I liked the sound of that option best. I just needed to figure out how to do it and we were less than ten minutes from Uncle's Jim's house. Since they didn't know where we were headed, I could use that to our advantage.

Uncle Jim is an ex-marine sniper who knows how to set a trap better than anyone, so I called and told him we were being chased by some maniac in a SUV and asked for his help. I knew I could trust him with my life and he didn't let me down. He told me to get everyone to his house as soon as possible.

I kept an eye on the SUV as we made our way into Prospect. I wasn't sure what Uncle Jim had in mind for them, but I was about to find out. It was only a few more blocks until we reached his street. The SUV followed close behind as we turned into his upscale subdivision, but stopped short when I made the last turn onto Uncle Jim's quiet cul-de-sac.

Uncle Jim lives in a red brick two story on the cusp of the circle. As I pulled into his driveway, I felt a little uneasy about leading the SUV to my Uncle's home, but Uncle Jim knows what he is doing. We found him sitting on his covered porch dressed in his usual faded jeans and Harley t-shirt. His bare feet were crossed at the ankle and his right hand held a smoldering Cuban cigar. Don't ask me where he gets them. Lying across his lap was a hunting rifle intended for large game.

A hand carved staff he uses when an old injury is acting up was leaning against the brick wall. He managed to escape the Gulf War unharmed, but fell rock climbing in the Red River Gorge a few years back. He survived the fall, but broke his back and lost an eye. The doctors said he would never walk again. Of course, Uncle Jim proved them wrong.

Thanks to a lean muscular frame, he looks younger than his age. His hair is more pepper than salt, with only a touch of a receding hairline. He wears an eye patch over the missing socket like a proud pirate. The remaining blue-grey eye was locked onto the SUV idling on the street corner. It reminded me of a dangerous beast that couldn't make up its mind whether it should venture into the cul-de-sac or not.

Uncle Jim waited. The tension was thick. I

wondered what would happen next. Of all the things I imagined, it sure wasn't what happened. A splash of rainbow descended from the heavens, squawking "Death from Above" and splattered bird shit all over the SUV's windshield. It was Dad's crazy macaw. That's all it took for the mighty beast to tuck tail and run. Of course, the sight of Uncle Jim's high-powered rifle might have had something to do with it too.

I suspected we weren't finished with the SUV, but it was a welcome relief to see it leave. Uncle Jim flashed his Cheshire cat grin and shouted Generalissimo. I stuck my left arm out the window and waved.

Ginny poked me in the side. Pain from the broken rib shot through me like a jolt of madness, but I liked her touch all the same.

"Generalissimo," she said with a broad smile.

"He says I might be a reincarnated Civil War general…he just can't figure out which one," I said sheepishly. "He's partial to Grant."

"Grant or Lee," she murmured. "But isn't your last name spelled Li?"

My mom's family is a distant relative of U.S. Grant on her mother's side. She and Uncle Jim have different fathers. He is lily white in a Nordic sort of way and every bit the Viking. My mom is half African-American.

Dad was Chinese and always said we were

related to a famous internal martial artist who lived a ridiculously long life. It was someone named Li Ching-Yun that the New York Times reported to have lived to be 256. I think my dad believed the crazy long life nonsense to be true just because it was in the newspaper. This very interesting bloodline explains my somewhat exotic, foreign look.

I was about to explain the nuances of my mixed heritage to Ginny, but was distracted by a flash of color and loud screech.

"Aaawk, Grant's a peckerwood."

It was dad's macaw with his usual greeting. The bird flew across the hood of the truck, up the windshield, and landed on the top. Hanging upside down he stuck his head in the driver's side window and looked around.

"I love you too bird," I grumbled.

He cocked his head at me.

"Aaawk, get a life," said Bird.

"Dad loved this bird," I said. "He belongs to me now, but I'm pretty sure he hates me."

"Aaawk, I belong to no one," squawked Bird. "Hate will be the death of us all."

Ginny looked mystified.

"Did he just respond to what you said?" asked Ginny. "I thought birds only mimic speech."

"Aaawk, such a pretty girl," said Bird.

Ginny cooed.

"Oh such a flirt," she said. "I like him."

"Aaawk, give us a kiss," squawked Bird.

"How cute, he just winked at me," said Ginny. "What's his name?"

"Bird," I answered.

"No really," said Ginny. "What's his name?"

"Dad always called him, Bird," I said. "I've never heard him called anything else."

"Humph," said Ginny.

Clearly she wasn't satisfied.

"Aaawk, my name is Senor Juan Ponce de Leon," said Bird.

Ginny asked, "Did he just say he is Ponce de Leon?"

"Aaawk, the one and only, pretty girl," said Bird.

"It's news to me," I said.

Uncle Jim limped over to the truck.

He handed Bird a peanut and said, "That's enough, Bird."

Then he opened the truck door, pulled me out, and gave me a bear hug. I winced as pain shot through my ribs. Uncle Jim doesn't miss anything and noticed when I stiffened from his embrace. He leaned back until I was at arm's length and looked me in the eyes to make sure we were good.

Satisfied, he looked me up and down, only pausing a moment to take in the blood stains.

He knew I was there for a reason, but waited for me to begin an explanation.

"We should talk before we call the police," I said.

He nodded his head and then shifted his one-eyed gaze to Ginny. A slow easy smile spread across his face.

"Don't pay any attention to that crazy fluff of feathers," he said. "I'm Jim."

"Aaawk, not crazy," said Bird.

Uncle Jim took a lazy swipe at Bird, who flew off squawking, "Aaawk, PETA alert! Someone call 9-1-1."

Ginny smiled at Uncle Jim and said, "I think you hurt his feelings. I'm Ginny."

"Don't let him fool you," said Uncle Jim. "That bird is tough as nails. Girl, you look just like your father."

If Ginny was surprised that Uncle Jim knew her father she didn't let on.

Instead, she said, "Well except for my dark hair, green eyes, and assorted girl parts."

Uncle Jim flashed a wolfish grin and said, "Your girl parts are welcome in my home. Who's your friend there?"

"This is Padma Ganesha," said Ginny. "He's my guest. I invited him to America to talk about his book. He was speaking tonight at the Center when someone tried to kill him. I think he was just about to reveal a secret about living a long life when it happened. We barely escaped with our lives thanks to Grant."

If Uncle Jim was surprised by any of this, he didn't show it.

Instead he gave Padma a long appraising look before saying, "I just lit the grill. Come out back and have a bite to eat. Grant, come inside for a moment, so I can look at that injury. Then, we can talk about your adventure over a cold drink."

We went inside where he cleaned the shallow gash with peroxide, and then protected it with gauze secured with first aid tape. I told everyone it was just a scratch, but it was a little more serious than that.

Uncle Jim is fond of telling people he has everything he needs in his own back yard. He is most proud of a 1970's style barbeque pit he built himself. Every evening the barbeque sends puffs of smoke into the sky as he grills burgers and sips cold beer. Its distinctive smell is a like a call to prayer for friends and neighbors, who religiously heed the summons.

Folks wander in from all four corners of the neighborhood. Gathering around the grill, they talk about the day's events and watch meat sizzle over hot coals. Later they sit in Adirondack chairs grouped under an ancient oak tree and watch the setting sun paint the clouds coral and blue. These are simple salt of the earth people sharing simple pleasures. There are no fences separating them. They move freely from yard to yard, house to house. It is a community in its truest sense.

As promised, Uncle Jim led us to the back yard where we settled into comfortable chairs and watched a squirrel gather acorns for the winter. Up and down the tree he went, never venturing onto the low hanging branch with the bug zapper. The distinctive sound of the zapper's grim work was balanced by the refreshing sound of bubbling water coming from Harrods Creek bordering the rear of the property.

The creek deepens enough at its mouth to provide a safe haven to area boaters who like to idle and party before emptying into the Ohio River. However, at this location it looks more like a mountain stream as it runs white over large flat rocks. This familiar scene calmed my nerves and the day's events began to feel surreal.

Uncle Jim disappeared into the house and then returned a few minutes later with tall glasses of bourbon and coke. He flashed his trademark confident smile and told Ginny it was for medicinal purposes only. She returned his smile, saying she could use all the medicine she could get.

Uncle Jim looked at me and winked.

"Grant", he said, "this one's a keeper."

Ginny beamed at Uncle Jim. I took another sip of the bourbon and relaxed into the scene playing out before me.

We sat quietly for a few minutes and listened to the evening's sounds. It felt good to not talk for a while, but then Uncle Jim spoke up. It was the last thing I wanted to talk about.

"Grant, you want to tell me what's going on?" asked Uncle Jim.

I stiffened and felt the first twinges of a headache.

Rubbing my temples I said slowly, "I don't know where to start."

"Do you remember calling me last night?" he asked. "You must have been about halfway through a bottle of tequila. You said you had won a big case for Wilbur Goth yesterday, but it didn't sound like much of a celebration. Instead, you got yourself fired. Your boss hung himself. Ch'ing is missing and you were chased here by gangsters with guns. Does that about cover it?"

"Actually, no, but I'm too wrung out right now to elaborate," I answered.

"Last night you said you said you were going to take some time off and search for Ch'ing in the Himalayas," said Uncle Jim. "Please tell me that was just crazy drunk talk. Ch'ing can take care of himself. You need to focus on your current predicament."

"Aaawk, lawyers get to lie and cheat for a living," squawked Bird. "Why do you want to give that up just to hang out in a drafty old monastery?"

"Bird, you're supposed to be guarding the perimeter," said Uncle Jim.

"Aaawk, eyes and ears on it," said Bird. "The perimeter is secured, sir."

I shook my head at Bird. He actually saluted Uncle Jim.

"Things can turn on a dime," I said. "Now, I may be the one who needs a criminal defense attorney."

"Your enemies have given you the gift of change," said Padma.

I had a flashback of Ch'ing teaching us an internal martial arts called, Baguazhang. The student is encouraged to overcome their natural resistance to change. High-level fighting techniques can be found in the transition moves, if the student has the courage to embrace change.

Ch'ing liked to spar ten-on-one and was always the last man standing. He moved like a whirling dervish teaching hidden techniques as he laid waste to all ten opponents. When the session was over, he'd look at our bodies on the floor and tell us we needed to do a better job of embracing change. We'd ask him how to do that, but he'd just shake his head and tell us to keep our feet moving next time.

Uncle Jim pulled me back from my reverie with a question.

"Do we need to talk to someone about representing you?" he asked.

"It would be best," I answered. "Lambers is dogging me over John's death and now there's...."

"You would never do such a thing!" said Ginny.

"No, but my word won't mean much under the circumstances," I said. "I need proof of my innocence or I'm in for a rough time."

"What kind of proof?" asked Ginny.

"I'm not sure, but Zeke Kruthers may hold the key," I answered.

"Isn't he the prosecutor you went up against in the Goth trial?" asked Uncle Jim.

I nodded.

"What's he have to do with John's death?" asked Uncle Jim.

I shook my head.

I filled them in on my meeting with Zeke at Ed's tavern.

"Do you have any idea what was in that envelope?" asked Ginny.

"Not a clue," I said.

"But you think it upset John enough he took

his own life?" asked Uncle Jim.

"That's what Kruthers seems to think," I answered.

Uncle Jim knows me well.

"You think Kruthers is right, don't you?" asked Uncle Jim.

I nodded grimly.

"Do you think this has anything to do with the murder at the Center?" asked Ginny.

I thought about the hug she gave Pony Tail and shrugged.

"Wait a minute...you mentioned a gunman earlier, but you didn't say anything about someone getting killed at the Center," said Uncle Jim.

"A security guard was stabbed," I said. "He was a friend of Eric's. A biker named Tiny."

"The leader of the Dragons," asked Uncle Jim.

I nodded.

"I had a run in with the murderer," I said. "He broke a couple of my ribs and then escaped."

"The Dragons will be out for blood," said Uncle Jim. "To bad he got away."

"I wished I had caught him," I said. "It all happened so fast. I went after him with the murder weapon. My prints are all over it."

"That's not good," said Uncle Jim in his best deadpan voice.

At this point, I don't think anything I said could have fazed him.

"This is bad, very bad," I said.

"We need to find the murderer," said Uncle Jim. "What did he look like?"

I shrugged.

"I didn't get a good look at his face," I said. "He wore a hooded monk's robe. I just saw a monk. They all look the same to me."

Padma snorted.

"Ch'ing will not be happy to hear you weren't more observant than that," said Uncle Jim. "Have you called the police?"

"I know I should talk to them about all of this, but I would prefer to get proof of my innocence first," I answered.

Uncle Jim nodded.

"What were you doing at the Center?" he asked.

"Working as a bodyguard," I answered.

He looked astonished.

"Bodyguard…who were you protecting?" he asked.

"Padma," I answered.

Uncle Jim raised an eyebrow.

"I am a simple monk," said Padma. "I have no need for a bodyguard."

"You didn't request protection," asked Uncle Jim.

Padma shook his head.

"Eric hired me," I said. "The strange thing about it is that his client specifically asked for me."

"Who are they and why you?" asked Uncle Jim.

I shrugged and turned to Ginny.

"Since your company sponsored this event, maybe you know something about the security arrangements," I asked.

She shook her head.

I sighed.

"Eric is looking into it," I said. "We should know something soon."

There was a flutter of feathers as Bird landed softly on Padma's shoulders. Bird looked lovingly at Padma and then gently rubbed his beak against the monk's cheek. Padma welcomed the comforting gesture, but looked like he was exhausted and fading fast.

In a tired voice he said, "It was a long journey from Bhutan and I must rest now."

Uncle Jim turned to Padma and asked, "Do you have any enemies?"

"Enemy...friend...two sides of the same coin," answered Padma.

The corners of Uncle Jim's mouth tightened, "You don't give straight answers to simple questions, do you? Why is that?"

Bird inched closer to Padma's cheek and glared at Uncle Jim. Padma reached up and gently smoothed his ruffled feathers, stroking from the back of the neck downward to the tip of his tail.

"Easy my friend," whispered Padma.

Ginny reached out and placed a soothing hand on Uncle Jim's forearm.

"Padma came all the way from Bhutan at my request," she said. "He planned to reveal an ancient secret. Someone tried to stop him."

"What secret?" asked Uncle Jim.

Padma smiled gently before answering, "Something that will change everything."

Uncle Jim shook his head, "You're not going to tell us, are you?"

"Now is not the time," replied Padma. "Be patient. Events must run their course."

"Run their course…people are dead and they're trying to kill us," I growled.

Uncle Jim looked thoughtful and nodded toward the house.

"Padma, you can use the bedroom at the end of the hall," said Uncle Jim. "I'll show you the way. I better call a few friends at the station and see what I can find out. Just sit tight until we figure out what to do next."

Bird stayed glued to Padma's shoulder as he followed Uncle Jim into the house. In the fading light, he looked like a strange two-headed beast.

CHAPTER 18

According to Ch'ing, at the end of each day, the immortals gather in the coral colored clouds to party. He promised I would see them when my heart is ready. I never watch a sunset without hoping for a glimpse of Dad. This sunset was different. On this evening, I watched the coral hues gather around Ginny.

As the color faded in the heavens, the last of the restless birds settled in for the night. Frogs began their nightly mating ritual, croaking to each other on the banks of Harrods Creek. Crickets marked territory with dueling chirps and the bug zapper fried insects unlucky enough to be lured into its purple glow. After all that had happened, it felt surreal to be sitting at Uncle Jim's like it was any other day.

When the first star appeared low in the sky, Ginny turned her glass and swallowed the last of the highball. She looked hesitant and when she finally spoke, it was tentative.

"Do you mind if I ask you a question?" she said.

This question usually triggered a red flag for

me, but not this time. I wanted us to open up with each other…I wanted to open myself to her.

"I don't mind," I answered.

"Do you regret that you listened to my mom and stayed away from me?" she asked.

It took a bit before I could formulate an answer without giving in to the great sadness that I lived with everyday. Still, my eyes burned with tears, but I didn't try to hide them from her.

"Yes, I regret it," I said. "The hardest thing I've ever done was watch her beat you without lifting a hand to stop it and then watch you walk out of my life."

"We were just little kids," said Ginny.

"I should have done something to stop her," I said.

"This isn't on you, Grant," said Ginny. "It's all my fault."

"What do you mean?' I asked.

"I was curious," she said. "I started the whole thing.'

I wasn't following her meaning at first, but then it hit me. She started the game of show-n-tell, but I didn't blame her. I never once blamed her. I always blamed myself for not standing up to her mother, for not protecting Ginny from her mother. It's true I was afraid of her mother, but all those years I stayed away, not because I was afraid of her mother, but because I wanted to protect Ginny.

"No one is to blame," I said.

There was confusion in Ginny's eyes, that quickly shifted to hope.

"Assigning blame has never solved anything," agreed Ginny. "We need to stop living in the past and move forward with our lives."

That's exactly what I was thinking and nodded.

"I visited your mother today," I said.

Ginny's hands flew to her mouth. Her brow was pinched and her eyes were filled with alarm. I waited until she recovered from the shock and understanding replaced the alarm.

"You wanted closure, didn't you?" she asked.

I nodded.

"I needed to let her know that she can't stop me from speaking to you, ever again," I said.

"How did it go?" she asked.

"About like you would expect," I said with a wry smile.

"She is a difficult person," said Ginny.

"Your mother was baking when I arrived," I said. "She was expecting to see you at her door, not me."

The amusement in her eyes disappeared. It was replaced with something dark and terrible. Her gaze dropped to her lap. I couldn't see her face to read it, but I sensed she needed comforting. It wasn't my thing, but something drew me to her side.

After a false start, I put a stiff arm around her. Unsure what to expect in return, I was relieved when she buried her face in my chest. She started to cry. I wanted to say something comforting, but nothing came to mind. Instead, I stroked her hair and just held tight until she stopped.

"I think she means well, but she's a nightmare," said Ginny.

After my talk with Kinsey, I wasn't sure her mother meant well. She seemed backward and filled with hate. Ginny's mother was religious in a way that bordered on fanatical. After hearing about the backward way the Taliban treated women in Afghanistan, I sometimes think of people like her mother as America's Taliban.

"Dad was nothing like Mom," said Ginny. "Dad was warm and loving. When she started one of her tirades, he would find a gentle way to diffuse her anger. Soon we would all be laughing and making plans to do something silly. He was a shining light on a dark night."

I remembered the gossip when Ginny's dad disappeared. Some said he ran away with another woman and just left his family to fend for themselves.

"What happened to your dad?" I asked.

"I don't know all of the details, but they argued about a trip to the Amazon Rainforest," she said. "Mother didn't want him to go. Before he left, he told me he had to do something that would change everything. He promised me he wouldn't be gone long, but he lied. I never saw him again."

"Do you have any idea what happened?" I asked.

"They say his plane crashed somewhere over the jungle," she answered. "The day we got the news my mother beat me with one of Dad's belts because my shorts showed too much leg. It was a hot day, but I changed into long pants and sleeves to appease her."

The beating I witnessed was not an isolated incident. Ginny's mother is abusive and she had been left alone with her. The realization that I could have helped brought the tears back. I resisted the urge to hide them, and instead, just let them have their way with me.

At least I had Uncle Jim and Ch'ing after I lost my parents. I couldn't imagine what it was like for her...alone with someone like that. To take my mind off her mother, I took a deep breath and tried to clear my head. Instead, I got a whiff of her intoxicating scent.

"It must have been tough after he left," I said.

She nodded.

"I wanted to placate her, so I dressed conservatively during my high school years," said Ginny. "You might even say, old fashioned. It didn't work. She got worse, instead of better. Eventually, I just lost myself."

"Old fashioned…you've definitely changed," I said. "How did that happen?"

Ginny bit her lip. She looked torn…as if she wasn't quite sure she could trust me. Finally, she made up her mind and answered.

"You know, I never had a date in high school," she said. "Instead, I poured myself into books and it paid off with scholarships. When it was time for college, I picked a school as far away from my mother as possible. I figured it would be harder for her to get to me in California."

"As soon as I got to Stanford, I set out to reinvent myself…to find myself," said Ginny. "I didn't have much money, so I started redesigning my old clothes and everyone started noticing."

"The other co-eds loved them and wanted to know where I bought them," she said. "They were trust-fund kids. I was embarrassed and didn't want to tell them the truth about my circumstances, so I avoided their questions. At least for a while, but they wouldn't stop pestering me until I finally confessed."

"I thought that would be the end of our

friendships, but they were really cool about it," said Ginny. "In fact, they were so impressed with my talent; they begged me to redesign their designer clothes. It surprised me. I didn't take them seriously until they offered to pay me."

"My designs were all the rage on campus," said Ginny. "Thanks to the power of social media, it spread like a virus to other campuses. Before long, I was running a small, but thriving business."

"By my junior year at Stanford, the business had grown to the point that I employed over a hundred workers, mostly women," she said. "Emerald Allure had arrived and me…well I found myself."

"Sounds like you're mother actually helped you in a back-handed sort of way," I said.

Ginny frowned, "I suppose so, but if it wasn't for Marguerite, I don't think I would have survived."

"Who's Marguerite?" I asked.

"She was my nanny," answered Ginny. "Mother wanted a good Hispanic woman to keep me on the straight and narrow while she was at work. I think she assumed Marguerite was Catholic, but she wasn't. Marguerite followed a more ancient path. Instead of bible study, she taught me to open my mind to the mystery of nature."

"The mystery of nature," I murmured. "That's a subject Ch'ing often talked about."

Ginny's smile was gentle. Her voice was soft.

"Marguerite was compassionate, like Dad," she said. "She also provided a soothing buffer from my mother's episodes."

"What happened to her?" I asked.

"I don't know," said Ginny. "We've stayed in touch and planned to meet for lunch yesterday, but she never showed. That's not like her at all."

"Odd, Ch'ing disappeared yesterday too," I said.

"Do you think there is a connection?" she asked.

I shrugged.

"You are very lucky to have both Uncle Jim and Ch'ing in your life," she said.

"He and Uncle Jim like to slap each other on the back and tell me what a good job they did raising me," I said. "Despite my present circumstances, I tend to agree."

Nodding toward the house she said, "I like your Uncle Jim. He's good people."

"He's always been there for me," I said. "I have been blessed to have him in my life."

"He seems worried about you," she said.

"He thinks I've lost my way," I said.

"Have you?" she asked.

"It's possible," I answered.

"What do you meant?' she asked.

I felt like she could be trusted, so I told her the truth.

"I hope I don't sound like an egomaniac, but I've always felt like there is an important role I have to play in the course of world events," I said.

She looked surprised, but quickly recovered.

"That's exactly how I feel, but I thought I was just compensating for my home life," she said.

"Are you satisfied with the direction you've taken in your life?" I asked.

She took a few breaths to give it some thought, before answering.

"As you have no doubt gathered, I stumbled into my line of work," she said.

"Me too," I said.

"I was undecided about a major at Stanford," she said. "When the clothes started selling, I knew I needed business skills, so I started taking business classes."

"Clearly, you have a talent for business," I said.

"Talent is good, but I believe a person needs a worthy life goal," she said.

"Have you found yours?" I asked.

She shook her head.

"Not exactly," she answered. "I have worthy

goals, but haven't found the big one yet."

"What do you mean?" I asked.

"I'm working to restore balance as best I can," she said.

"In what way?" I asked.

"Take for example, the corporate glass ceiling," she said. "I hire desperate women and give them the skills they need to succeed. I help them find their purpose...their focus. They have the opportunity to rise in my company based solely upon their performance."

"That is certainly a worthy goal," I agreed. "Do you have any idea what the big one might be?"

She shook her head.

"It's elusive," she said. "Sometimes I wake in the middle of the night with the feeling that it is nearby, but I can't quite get a picture of it."

"I know what you mean," I said.

"You're a successful attorney," she said. "Is your destiny tied to the law?"

"I'm not sure," I said. "Lately, I've gotten a look at the business side of a law practice and it's not as noble as I'd like, but like you, I stumbled into it and am trying to use it as a vehicle for something bigger."

"How did you stumble into it?" she asked.

"For as long as I can remember, I wanted to be a writer," I said. "I imagined writing great books that lived forever in the imagination of readers."

Ginny looked surprised at my answer.

"Then why did you go to law school?" she asked.

"Uncle Jim wanted me to go to college, but he didn't have the money to pay for it," I answered. "When I was offered a scholarship to play football at West Point he was thrilled. He took to calling me General Li…sometimes General Grant. Later, it was just Generalissimo, but he always said it with pride."

"I heard him call you that," she said. "I like it."

"Thing was…I didn't want to play football anymore and I sure didn't want to disappoint him," I said.

"How did you get out of that bind?" she asked.

"Badly…I'll never forget the day I told him I wasn't going to take the scholarship," I said. "Uncle Jim looked so damn disappointed. He sat there at the kitchen table looking tired and beaten. I had never seen him like that. To his credit, he shook it off and asked me what I planned to do with my life."

"I told him I still planned to go to college and had even thought about going to law school," I said. "He lit up like a Christmas tree, slapped me on the back and told me he was proud of me."

"It was true I planned to go to college, but I don't know why I said that about law school," I said. "The thought never crossed my mind. Afterwards, he kept going on and on about law school and I didn't have the heart to tell him it was a weird slip of the tongue."

Ginny looked thoughtful and said, "You did it for him and still became a rock star lawyer."

"It was important to him and that's what love does," I said.

"Love puts another before self," she said. "So many people seem to get that backwards."

Light shot up my spine and exploded in my head like a Fourth of July display. Despite the evening's heat, I massaged the goose bumps on my arms.

"Yes, but we can never sacrifice the prime directive to live our own lives on our own terms," I said.

Ginny nodded in agreement.

"Rock star lawyer," I said. "Besides Uncle Jim, you might just be my first and only groupie."

"Do you have room for anyone else?" she asked.

I was about to tell her that there is plenty of room in my life for her, but we were interrupted by Uncle Jim.

"What are you two love birds talking about?" asked Uncle Jim.

"The mysteries of life and love," answered Ginny.

"Good luck with that," said Uncle Jim. "Speaking of problems, we have something more immediate at hand that requires our attention."

"Let me guess," I said. "The police have a witness and they are planning to charge me with John's murder."

Uncle Jim looked surprised.

"How did you know?" he asked.

I shrugged.

"I bet it's John's secretary," I said.

"They didn't say," he replied. "We need to clear this up as quickly as possible. It's always best to nip things like this in the bud."

"I'm trying," I said. "I even rummaged through John's office to see if I could find out why he killed himself."

"What did you find?"

"Nothing," I answered. "All I found was a slip of paper.

"What did it say?" asked Uncle Jim.

I smacked my forehead.

"I never read it," I said. "Lambers showed up and drilled me with questions."

I shoved my hands into my pockets, but all I felt was my phone. Of course it wouldn't be there, because I was wearing different pants. The slip of paper was still in my suit trousers. I needed to see what was written on that paper.

CHAPTER 19

Ginny refused to be left behind. To my dismay, she insisted on seeing where I lived. I have to admit I was not looking forward to showing her my crappy apartment and tried every excuse I could think of to avoid it. None of them worked. I learned she can be very strong willed and must confess that I caved in when it became apparent she intended to get her way.

To soften the blow, I took the long route through Cherokee Park. It was designed in the late 1800's by Frederick Law Olmstead after he finished work on New York's Central Park. As you can imagine, it's a world class park and unlike my apartment, it is beautiful. I hoped it would fill Ginny's mind with nature's images and leave very little room for hookah bars and beat up second hand furniture.

Once inside of the apartment, she stood in the middle of the room and took it all in. After what seemed like a ridiculously long inspection she finally spoke.

"Living above a hookah bar does have a certain charm," she said.

In that moment, I knew I loved her all over again. The place was a dump and we both knew it. She was trying to alleviate my embarrassment and that meant a lot to me.

Relieved I said, "When I left Cynthia, I needed to find a place to stay. This was never intended to be more than temporary."

"Where do you see yourself?" she asked.

I wanted to tell her I saw myself married to her with a house full of kids living the fairy tale of happily ever after, but couldn't bring myself to say something that corny out loud.

"A home should…"

I was interrupted by a harsh male voice coming from the doorway behind me.

"He doesn't give a shit about marriage," he said.

Standing at the threshold was a big hairy guy with the Harley Davidson logo tattooed across his chest. He was wearing dirty jeans and a black leather vest worn over bare skin. A pack of Marlboro's jutted from his jean's pocket. The vest displayed the colors of Dragon's Gate motorcycle club. His black motorcycle boots showed signs of heavy wear at the heels and toes.

Huge hands hung at his sides, opening and closing spasmodically. His finger nails were outlined with black grease. Hard eyes glared at me from a weather beaten face. He was a rough looking man wearing an unhappy expression. This did not bode well.

"Who are you?" I asked.

"I'm your worst nightmare," he growled.

"Maybe, but a man who doesn't know his enemy is doomed to a life of regret…assuming he manages to survive his ignorance," I said.

He sneered.

"What kind of stupid fool are you anyway?" he asked.

"I'm the guy who may have to decide whether you live or die," I answered calmly.

Doubt flashed in his eyes and then passed quickly. His right hand swept to his low back, but I didn't wait to find out what kind of weapon he had. Instead, I closed the gap between us in an instant and jabbed him in the solar plexus. The air left his lungs and he crumbled to the ground desperately trying to catch his breath.

I rolled him over and removed a 9mm jammed down the crack of his ass. I didn't stop there and quickly found the knife hidden in his inner vest pocket and the snubbed nose revolver stashed in his boot. Once I was satisfied he was disarmed, I sat him up, and rubbed his back behind the heart until he calmed himself and found some air.

"Let's try this one more time," I said. "Who are you?" I asked.

"My name is Gil," he answered.

"Why are you here Gil?" I asked.

"Because you slept with my wife last night," he answered.

"Why do you think that?" I asked.

"Because she came home without her wedding ring," he answered.

The big lug started to sob. I comforted him as best I could until the sobbing finally stopped.

"Look Gil, I didn't..."

I was interrupted by Ginny, who held a gold wedding band in her hand.

"What is engraved inside of her ring?" she asked.

"True love," he answered.

Ginny handed him the ring and then turned to me.

"The one thing I can't tolerate is a liar," she said.

Then she walked out. Gil stood up, brushed himself off and followed her. But he stopped for a moment, turned, and looked at me with big sad eyes, before shaking his head and walking away with more dignity than I could have mustered under the circumstances. I was stunned to say the least.

It took a few minutes for me to process what had just happened. When I finally realized that Ginny didn't understand that I had never slept with Eve, I started after her, but the minute my foot stepped outside the door I was slammed faced down onto the ground and my arms were pinned behind my back. I felt a knee jam into my spinal cord as handcuffs were roughly slapped onto my wrists.

When I tried to get a look at my assailant, he pressed my face into the floor and barked for me to stay still as all hell broke loose around me. Armed men stormed the stairs and poured into the hallway. Doors were opened and then slammed shut as they yelled things like "clear" to each other. I realized I was in the middle of a full-on swat team raid. This could not be good.

They packed me into a paddy wagon with four armed guards and hauled me downtown to Louisville Metro Police headquarters. I was left alone for about an hour before the interrogation began. I have to say, it's a lot easier to ask the questions, than to answer them. The interrogation was grueling. They came at me in waves… men, women, young and old with assorted titles from the CDC, Homeland Security, and Louisville Metro Police.

I couldn't understand why I was being treated like a terrorist. Of course, no one would explain why the CDC and Homeland Security were interested in a homicide. Instead, they poked me with needles, drawing several vials of blood, which seemed weird, and repeatedly threatened to throw me into prison. When that didn't work, they offered me leniency if I told them everything. That was easy since I knew nothing. I had nothing to hide, but I was concerned about my prints on Tiny's murder weapon.

It would have been smarter to hold my tongue until I had an attorney present. Even I had enough sense to know that I couldn't represent myself, but I really wanted to help find the killer. So, I held nothing back.

Still they weren't satisfied, so they threw me a curve ball when Rose entered the room. It sent me reeling into the past.

***

I flashed back to myself sitting in the third row of Sister Mary John's class. Her thin frame was swallowed in a nun's traditional black habit. During the first week of school she told us she was married to Jesus, but I didn't believe her. Because of her hawkish nose and shrill voice, I was certain she was the Wicked Witch of the West and who would want to marry her? Definitely not Jesus, who I'd been taught was some kind of superhero.

With a spooky air of mystery she told us,

"God knows all things. That means you don't have any secrets from God. He knows when you've been good or bad."

Danny's hand shot up. Danny's hand was always shooting up.

"Is God Santa Claus?" asked Danny.

She sighed.

"Daniel, wait until you are called upon before you speak," said Sister Mary John. "God is more than Santa Claus. This means that God is omniscient."

She paused dramatically, as if she had revealed a great secret to us that needed time to sink in.

Then she added, "He is also omnipotent. Does anyone know what that means?"

We stared at her with blank faces. Even Danny's hand stayed down. She sighed once again.

"It means God is all powerful," she said. "He can do whatever he wants, whenever he wants."

Danny's hand shot up once more.

"Does that mean he leaps tall buildings like Superman?" asked Danny.

"God does not leap over buildings," said Sister Mary John. "He uses his power to create. God created everything, even you Daniel. Last but not least, God is Omnipresent. That means

God is everywhere at the same time. God is even in each one of you."

I thought if God is in me, then maybe I have super powers too. Maybe I can be smart like Einstein or a superhero someday. As I sat there pondering this amazing realization, Sister Mary John's class was interrupted by a knock. Her eyes shot daggers toward the door and then quickly softened. The principal stood in the doorway apologizing for interrupting her class. She then asked Sister Mary John to excuse me from class.

I was being called to the principal's office. I had never been to her office. As everybody knows, only the bad kids are sent there. I went from superhero to scared little boy in seconds. I was terrified. It got worse when I saw the police woman with her.

Every one of my misdeeds ran through my mind. Maybe the Fat Lady told the policeman I was a nasty little boy and they were taking me to jail. I didn't want to go to jail. My legs didn't seem to work so good as I shuffled toward the police woman. I kept my eyes on the floor, not daring to look into her face.

"Grant, look at me," said the police woman.

When I looked into her face, she didn't look angry. Instead, I only saw sadness. When she spoke it was with a gentle voice. She told me her name was Rose and she had some bad news…my mother was hurt and in the hospital, but my dad was in heaven now.

***

Rose Bloom had been that young police woman and was now in her mid-forties. She had aged well. Her auburn hair shared space with a few streaks of grey at the temples, and her grey eyes were framed by a faint hint of crow's feet, but she was still a beautiful woman. She no longer wore a patrolman's uniform. Instead she was dressed in jeans and a navy blue sport jacket over a white blouse.

Rose looked grief stricken and angry, which didn't quite mesh with the situation, unless I was missing something. It occurred to me that she almost seemed to be in shock, but was making a tremendous effort to keep it together. It didn't make any sense. She was her normal self yesterday when we searched Ch'ing's house.

"Has Ch'ing showed up yet?" she asked.

"Not yet," I answered. "Rose, I didn't kill Tiny."

"Why were you at the Center?" asked Rose.

Here we go again. I had been over this dozens of times already.

"Eric called and offered me a job," I said.

"You had just won a big trial for Wilbur Goth," said Rose. "Why would you take a job the next day as a bodyguard?"

"I was placed on a leave of absence pending an investigation into John's death, so despite the win yesterday, I'm currently unemployed," I answered.

"Do you have any bodyguard experience?" she asked.

"No, I don't," I answered.

"Then why did he send you?" she asked.

"I asked him that and he said they specifically asked for me," I answered.

"Who asked for you?" said Rose.

"I asked Eric that too, but he doesn't know," I answered. "Someone else at his company took the call. He's looking into it."

"Let's go over the shooting," she said.

I ran through it once again, telling her everything I remembered about it.

The door opened and Detective Lambers walked into the room. He moved off to my left and glared at me without speaking.

"I've been expecting you, Lambers," I said.

"That's Detective Lambers, punk," he said.

"What you are is a man who isn't fit to wear a badge," I said.

He came for me. Rose pulled him from my throat and then two uniformed officers removed him from the room.

"Seriously Rose, he needs to get some help," I said.

She sighed and ran her finger tips through her hair.

"This is important, Grant, what aren't you telling us?" asked Rose.

"We've been over this dozens of times already," I answered. "I saw Pony Tail reach for his weapon. I killed the lights. There were two shots fired. I was hit. I fled with Ginny. Padma followed us. There was a second shooting in the parking lot. We drove to Uncle Jim's. The SUV followed us, but left when they saw Uncle Jim armed with a hunting rifle."

"What did you see after the lights were turned off?" asked Rose

I shook my head.

"What was the audience doing?" asked Rose.

Funny thing about memory, we have a tendency to focus on the things we think are important. Those are the things we recall the easiest. Everything else is forgotten. Except, nothing is ever really forgotten. It is stored away and ignored, but never really forgotten.

"They were fighting to get to the exits, but there was a logjam at the doors," I said. "They were pounding on the doors. It was if they had been locked inside, but that's not possible."

The blood drained from Rose's face. She sat across from me in shocked silence, not breathing. It seemed like an eternity before she caught her breath.

"The doors were closed," I repeated. "They couldn't get them open."

Rose's hands were trembling. Her eyes haunted. I placed a reassuring palm over her shaking hand. She broke down.

Between sobs she repeated over and over, "Oh my God...my baby...my poor baby."

It seemed to be confirming something she already knew. Had something happened to Kim? How was she involved in all of this? Before her breakup with Uncle Jim, Rose and her daughter, Kim, lived with us for several years.

Kim was like a sister to me and if she had been injured during the shooting at the Center, I would never forgive myself. I should have called the police when I found Tiny's body.

"Has something happened to Kim?" I asked.

"The Center...she was at the Center..."

The door to the interrogation room clanged open and a deep voice bellowed, "Get her out of here...now!"

Two burly men with buzz cuts stormed in, grabbed Rose under the arms and drug her from the room. I expected the door to close behind them, but instead a tall grey haired man with cold blue eyes stepped into the room. He was dressed in a military uniform. I didn't know how to read the soldier's rank, but his chest sported an impressive collection of medals.

Mr. Medals strode across the room in two strides and then stopped within inches. He was well within my personal space which would have made most people uncomfortable. Since I'm comfortable with close range combat, it didn't bother me. Arm's reach just means I have less of a gap to bridge when the fight starts.

I guessed his height to be six four or five. In my seated position, it was a bit of a strain to tilt my head up and look him in the eye, but I did and I wished I hadn't.

The room suddenly felt cold. Goose bumps appeared on my arms. As hard as I tried I couldn't stop shivering. It probably only lasted ten seconds, but it seemed much longer. Stillness followed. I didn't dare blink. This man had seen so much death, it had become who he is.

Finally, Mr. Medals asked, "Where is she?"

It was the last thing I expected. What did he want with Ginny? Even if I knew, I wouldn't have told him. So instead of answering I continued my vigil.

Very deliberately, Mr. Medals opened a manila folder, removed a photograph and slid it across the table. I guess I expected him to say something, but he didn't.

I cut my eyes to the photograph and saw a man wearing a wife beater, combat boots and military style trousers. He posed in front of a dust covered Humvee with muscular arms folded across his chest. I guessed him to be about 5'8". His brown hair was cropped short and a combat hardened face was partially obscured by aviator glasses.

Shrugging my shoulders I deliberately pushed the photograph back to him and waited. It was getting easier to look into death's face without feeling sick to my stomach.

He studied me closely. Maybe he saw something, I don't know, but he tapped the photo with his forefinger as if to say, "Look again."

Something was vaguely familiar about the soldier in the photo, but I couldn't get my head around it. My mind grasped at fleeting images that flashed through it at lightning speed, like those subliminal messages encoded in video that they tried to outlaw years ago because of its alarming ability to brainwash us all.

I was really close to putting my finger on it when Mr. Medal's fist slammed the table and he shouted, "Where is she, boy?"

She? He seemed to be referring to the photograph of the soldier. It was then that I realized the soldier was a woman.

My dad was Chinese and mother was mulatto. Most people don't have a clue about my ethnicity. They just think I am exotic. I was only one-quarter African-American, but calling me boy was enough to piss me off. It made me hot enough I was willing do something stupid, like kick this jerk's ass.

That was exactly what I was about to do when an authoritative voice ordered, "Stop right there."

My unwavering gaze was locked unto Mr. Medals, but his eyes faltered for the first time. It was a small victory, but one I desperately needed under the circumstances. There are pivotal moments in a life when everything seems to turn on a dime. This was one such moment. Mr. Medals released me and turned to the voice.

CHAPTER 20

It was an orator's voice, powerful enough to carry to the back of an auditorium without assistance from a microphone. Deep and rich, it commanded one minute and seduced the next. I knew it well. The saving voice belonged to Laurence Filmore, my criminal law professor.

He was a tall man with a full head of white hair that draped his proud face like a lion's mane. He was dressed in a bright Hawaiian shirt covered with pink pineapples, Bermuda shorts, and lime green flip flops. At the moment he didn't look much like an attorney, but it was the weekend, after all. Come to think of it, he didn't look like he'd just come from church services either.

Despite the lack of a proper lawyer costume, Filmore filled the room with his presence. It was more than charisma, although he had that in abundance. This man commanded respect.

In addition to teaching young men and women to be effective litigators, he was Louisville's top criminal defense attorney. His success was legendary. He never lost a case. The very mention of his name causes law enforcement officials to cringe.

Law hadn't always been his career path. Following his graduation from the Naval Academy he rose to the rank of admiral. He brought his skills to bear in two wars, but shifted gears when his son was wrongfully convicted of a brutal rape and sentenced to fifteen years in prison thanks to a forced confession.

Filmore earned his law degree from Georgetown University during a tour of duty in Washington, D.C. The Navy wasn't willing to let him go and when he insisted on practicing law, President Bush convinced him to remain in the naval reserves.

Filmore and I became friends thanks to a program the law school called "Dining with a Professor." Each of the law school professors would invite a small group of students to their homes once a month and cook dinner for us. I selected Filmore because he reminded me of Uncle Jim. In fact, it turned out Uncle Jim had served under him on some secret mission during the Gulf War. Their history created a bridge that helped facilitate our relationship.

Mr. Medals knew who stood before him. I could see it in his eyes. It was also evident that he was weighing his options and not liking the outcome of any of them.

"Stand down," ordered Filmore.

Mr. Medals' jaw tightened. There was a flash of defiance in his eyes that Filmore moved to quash.

"You will not ask my client another question until I've had an opportunity to speak with him in private," said Filmore.

"You are interfering with my investigation," growled Mr. Medals.

"This young man is a murder suspect and you just tried to provoke him into a fist fight," said Filmore. "You're a Marine Colonel and you answer to me. This isn't Bagdad. Step away from my client."

"I was testing him," said Mr. Medals.

"You were trying to entrap him," said Filmore.

"I wanted to know if he really has the skills to survive an encounter with her," said Mr. Medals.

"Who is she?" asked Filmore.

"This investigation is classified, Admiral," answered Mr. Medals.

"Then, you're done here," said Filmore. "That's a direct order."

Mr. Medals deflated with a sharp hiss. His eyes scanned from side to side a couple of times as he quickly processed Filmore's order. When he spoke again, his tone was less combative…softer.

"There are other prints on the murder weapon," said Mr. Medals.

"The killer's prints…they belong to Pony Tail," I said.

Mr. Medals shook his head and pointed at the photograph on the table.

Filmore calmly walked to the table and picked up the photo. Recognition flickered in his eyes. His shoulders dropped a fraction of an inch and for the first time since his dramatic arrival he seemed unbalanced…less sure of himself.

"Kim Slotter was awarded the Congressional Medal of Honor for God's sake," said Filmore. "How could this happen?"

It wasn't so much a question directed at Mr. Medals. Instead, it seemed to be a private thought that somehow had managed to find voice. One of those slips of tongue that leaves us wondering if we really said that out loud. The problem was that Filmore never made mistakes. It was as if the photograph had put him in a place where he lost himself.

"Private sector," answered Mr. Medals with a hint of distaste as if that explained everything.

Filmore looked up from the photograph. The trance was broken, but he looked less commanding…more collaborative. Even though he knew me well, he studied me like a potential enemy. My life was in his hands and he appeared to be compromised. It scared me.

He was looking at me, but his next question was directed to Mr. Medals.

"She's one of yours, Colonel," said Filmore. "You trained her?"

"Yes, she's the best I've seen," said Mr. Medals. "This man could not have survived a knife fight with her."

"You've lost your objectivity in this investigation," said Filmore. "Stand down."

"I have to find her," repeated Mr. Medals. "It's a matter of national security."

"You're only protecting one of your own," said Filmore. "How is that a matter of national security?"

Mr. Medals shook his head and said, "That's classified."

"I am your superior officer," barked Filmore. "You will answer my question."

Mr. Medals cut his eyes to me.

"Not in front of the civilian," he said.

Filmore turned sharply toward the door.

"Follow me, Colonel," said Filmore.

They left me alone to ponder this strange turn of events. I had assumed Tiny's killer was Pony Tail, but it was Slotter. Before Rose was dragged from the room in tears, she was about to tell me something about Kim...it had to do with the Center.

Then, I thought about the swat team and the interrogation. The physicians from the CDC kept asking how I was feeling and whether I noticed any unusual odors at the Center. I told them I didn't smell anything other than gun powder. Why did they ask that and why was the CDC involved in a murder investigation?

Then, there was the full blown physical exam they put me through. It went way beyond the collection of evidence. Geez, they wore hazmat suits for heaven's sake, like I was hazardous or something.

Filmore's return interrupted my thoughts, but when I noticed his pale face and trembling hands, my fears returned with a vengeance. I desperately wanted to know what Mr. Medals told him and started to ask, but he shook his head. The police station had too many eyes and ears.

Motioning me to follow, he led me out of the building and to his black Cadillac parked in front of LMPD headquarters. I couldn't believe we were just walking out of there after all they put me through. Judging by the sun, it was early evening. I had been interrogated for nearly twenty-four hours and was exhausted, but ecstatic. I really thought they were going to lock me up and throw away the key.

Filmore didn't speak until we pulled into Uncle Jim's driveway.

"You need to be very careful, Grant," said Filmore.

"What is going on?" I asked.

"Something very dangerous," he answered. "That's all I can tell you. Try to get some rest. You look like crap. One more thing, stay out of the city."

His intention was clear. I was dismissed. Uncle Jim was waiting for me at the door, looking like a worried parent, so I thanked Filmore for his help and went to face my uncle.

I expected him to drill me with questions, but instead Uncle Jim pointed to the sofa and handed me a pillow. Grateful, I curled up on the couch and closed my eyes. I remember thinking too much had happened over the last couple of days and sleep would be impossible, but I did sleep. As I drifted off, the last thing I thought of was the Colt 45 tucked in Uncle Jim's belt. It was a comforting end to an insane day.

The smell of fresh coffee woke me from a nightmare. It wasn't the familiar one involving the Fat Lady. Maybe that demon had finally been laid to rest. This one was a new one and it was far worse. It involved mass murder, but thankfully, I couldn't remember the details.

I peeked out of the corner of my eye and into

a ray of light shining through the living room window. It was morning. My back was stiff from the soft cushions, but I was safe in Uncle Jim's house. A hand moved toward me, blocking the glare.

"Have you started having those dreams again?" asked Uncle Jim.

He offered a cup of coffee.

"This was something new," I murmured. "Maybe I've graduated to new terrors. How long was I out?"

"You slept about fourteen hours. It's Monday morning. Come join us for some breakfast."

"Us?" I asked.

"Padma showed up a few of hours before you," answered Uncle Jim. "It was kind of weird. I didn't hear a car drop him off. I'm not sure how he got here. When I asked him about it, he said he took a ride on a magic carpet."

"Showed up…didn't I leave him here Saturday night?" I asked.

"He slipped out of the house," said Uncle Jim. "I didn't even know he was gone."

Uncle Jim looked thoroughly disgusted with himself. Given his background in the Special Forces, I could understand why it bothered him that a monk was able to slip by him undetected.

I rubbed the sleep from my eyes and

followed him into the kitchen. Padma was sitting at the table drinking coffee. The guy never stops smiling. Geez, you'd think he would have to give his cheeks a rest once in a while.

Sausage gravy was bubbling on the stove. Bird was perched at his favorite spot on top of the refrigerator. The smell of homemade biscuits drifted from the oven. Jars of jelly and sorghum sat in the center of the table. It was a comforting scene.

"Aaawk, the jailbird is free," said Bird. "Did you make any new friends in the slammer? I'm surprised you can sit down."

"Hush bird," said Uncle Jim.

Oddly, it made me feel better. It was familiar. Bird gives me a hard time and Uncle Jim calls him out on it. You might call it a family tradition.

"Merry morning!" greeted Padma.

I'm not much of a morning person, but it felt good to be home. As Uncle Jim topped our cups with hot coffee, I had to smile at Padma's mug. There was a silhouette of a dancer with her leg hooked around a pole. He turned it so I could read the other side where it said, "Support a Single Mom."

"Good morning Padma," I said. "That's an interesting coffee mug."

His smiled widened.

"Isn't it lovely?" he asked.

"Ummm, yes it is," I answered. "Where did you get it?"

Padma nodded toward Uncle Jim.

"It was a gift from my doctor," said Uncle Jim.

I choked on my coffee. The spray made a huge mess. Sadly, a stream of it hit Bird, sending him squawking across the room in a flash of red, blue and yellow. He was very upset. Oh, the joy of revenge!

"She worked as a dancer to pay her way through medical school, and yes, she was a single mom," said Uncle Jim.

After I cleaned the mess, Uncle Jim filled mismatched plates with hot buttermilk biscuits and then poured sausage gravy over them. He sat a pitcher of orange juice and a gallon of whole milk in the center of the table. I rarely eat breakfast, but my stomach rumbled approval.

We finished our breakfast in silence. Uncle Jim was thoughtful. Padma was inscrutable. Bird focused on his morning bath and shooting me dirty looks every couple of minutes. I'm pretty sure I heard him grumble something about never getting the stains out of his feathers.

After the last dish was washed and put away, I excused myself and stepped outside for some fresh air. I needed time to think. Too much had happened too fast. The door squeaked opened behind me and Uncle Jim stepped out. He draped his arm across my shoulders and stood quietly next to me. I had a memory of him doing the same thing after my dad was killed. It was comforting.

A woodpecker searched for breakfast in the oak tree. Together, we scanned the ancient tree for a glimpse of him. Uncle Jim was a marine sniper. Even with one eye, he could see better than most.

He spotted the woodpecker first and said, "Do you see him, Grant? Look about half way up the tree, to the right. He's sitting about a third of the way out, on that branch."

Thanks to his directions, I found the woodpecker and said, "Yes, I see him now."

"I know it's corny, but I call him Woody," said Uncle Jim. "Bird hates him. He says all that knocking gives him a headache."

"He's such a drama queen," I said.

"Aaawk. Bird's a king. All hail the king."

I thought Bird was still inside. He must have slipped out with Uncle Jim. A few comebacks came to mind, but I didn't want to fuel Bird's foul disposition. Instead, I just watched Woody do his thing.

Padma appeared at my side. Funny, I was sure he didn't come out with Uncle Jim and I didn't hear the noisy door hinged. How does he keep doing these things? And the way he looks at me…it feels as if he can see into all of my dark places.

As if he had read my mind, Padma said, "You stand at the eight gates."

Eight gates…I've heard that expression before. Then, I had a flashback of myself standing on this very porch when I was eight years old. I was alone and crying. Earlier that day, a police woman had told me my dad had been killed in a hit-and-run motorcycle accident.

Then, I heard a voice. It was gentle and kind. It came from a man who wasn't much bigger than me. He told me his name was Ch'ing and that it is okay to be sad. He said sadness is one of the eight gates of change and, someday, I would stand at all eight gates. I didn't understand any of that, but he had gotten my attention when he had asked me if I wanted to learn Kung Fu.

I was brought back to the present by a ring from my cell. I glanced at the screen and saw it was an unknown caller. I never take those calls, but something told me I should this time. I'm glad I did. It was Ginny's voice I heard, but what she said sent a chill up my spine.

"I'm so scared, Grant. They have me. Please help."

CHAPTER 21

A man fights many battles in his lifetime, but the only one that really matters is the fight for something he is afraid to lose. It doesn't matter whether it's a person, thing, or the cherished notions he holds about himself. All that really matters is how he handles the fear.

Fear causes him to settle for less than he deserves. Settling for second best is never a viable option in an enlightened life. It is a darkness of spirit that reduces him to less than he is…a shadow of his true nature. Settling is a compromise with fear that never works out for the best in the end, because the purpose of life is to express his true nature.

Never chose the safe path when it requires you to choose something other than your true nature. Fear must be faced head-on with the determination to give it your best shot and enough resolve to accept whatever outcome fate holds for you.

Ch'ing taught me to remain calm in the face of danger by centering myself in the present. Hours of full contact sparring made it an absolute necessity. He would attack on multiple levels at blistering speed…hands, feet, hips, shoulders, elbows flying everywhere, seemingly, at the same time until the pain of the blows got my full attention.

All of those hours of training fell away at the sound of Ginny's plea for help. Before I could answer, I heard another voice…an icy cold voice. It sent a cold fear down into the pit of my stomach. The voice told me Ginny is as good as dead if I even think of calling the police. The voice told me to wait for further instructions that must be followed without exception or she will die a slow and painful death.

My knees buckled and I gripped the phone like it was some sort of lifeline. Once again, I felt the crippling terror of losing someone I love. There had been too much loss, already. Fear had arrived full force into my life.

I had to rescue her, but I was frozen in place by the terrible news I had just received. It was Padma who came to my rescue.

"Come sit with me, Grant," he said softly. "It is time for meditation."

Padma led us down the bank of Harrods Creek to a large flat rock at water's edge where he gracefully dropped into a perfectly balanced sitting position. Even though his back was ramrod straight, he didn't look stiff. Instead, he seemed completely relaxed. For such a heavy-set man, he was amazingly nimble.

In sharp contrast to Padma, I was bent like a bow...rigid and filled with anxiety. The phone call from Ginny had ended abruptly. My repeated call backs dropped without a single ring. I desperately wanted to know where she was and who had her. If Ginny was taken by Slotter, then she was in grave danger. The not-knowing was unbearable.

"Grant, it's time to get out of your head and come to your senses," said Padma.

I felt a flash of anger and said a little too harshly, "What the hell does that mean?"

My anger didn't last. It was instantly swallowed by the kindness in his eyes and just evaporated. I knew what he meant. It was time to quiet my worried thoughts and focus on the present moment. I really did try, but failed miserably. The last couple of days had been a nightmare that continued to plague me. My thoughts refused to be silenced.

With a graceful sweep of his arm Padma asked, "What do you see?"

I half-heartedly glanced around me and mumbled something about a creek. Like any good teacher, he enthusiastically praised my correct answer. I knew he was pulling my leg, but the silliness of his praise somehow managed to hook me. So, I took another look.

When the spring rains pour heavy, Harrods Creek is a wide stream full of boulders and white water. On this summer day, it carried less water and flowed more gently around the rocks with only a touch of white.

The far shore was lined with dogwoods, redbuds, and a sycamore or two. Twenty-feet downstream, a bushy-tailed red fox slipped quietly down the bank and took a sip of water. Two baby foxes followed close behind.

It is a rare treat to see a fox and a miracle to see a family enjoying one of the simple pleasures in life. The kids were more interested in play than water. They chased each other through the tall grass, darting back and forth in a joyful game of tag. Oddly, the fox family paid no attention to us until a splash sent them scurrying back into the safety of the woods.

The splash came from a small eddy behind the flat rock I was sitting on. A tail fin was sticking vertically out of the water. I had never seen anything like it. How does a fish do that?

Curious, I reached down and grabbed hold with my thumb and forefinger. You'd think the alarmed fish would dart away. But it didn't. So, I gave a little tug. Something pulled back, even harder. My competitive nature took over and I tugged back. The fish came out of the water, slipped through my fingers with a splash and swam away.

I thought that was the end of it, but an angry water moccasin popped its head out of the water and glared at me for ruining its meal. I jumped out of my skin. Snakes scare me and water moccasins are one of Kentucky's most poisonous varieties. Padma just laughed his ass off as I jumped to another rock.

"Real funny," I grumbled. "I hate snakes."

"You and Indiana Jones," giggled Padma.

Comparing me to Indiana Jones was a stretch, but it somehow made me feel better and I smiled for the first time that morning.

"Oh, you've found your humor," said Padma. "That's good. Connecting with your inner smile is what meditation is all about. If you can do that 24/7, especially during a crisis, then you will have discovered the secret of life."

His comments surprised me, so I said, "That's it...that's the meditation lesson. I thought we were going to sit in lotus posture and chant a mystical phrase or something."

Padma's only response was to do that laughing Santa thing he does. It was annoying at first, but suddenly I got it. A huge load lifted and light poured through me. Before long, I was laughing like Santa myself.

When the laughter subsided, he suggested I

take a moment to acknowledge the healing that had just taken place and to never forget the difference it can make in one's life. I can't explain it, but I suddenly had this overwhelming sense of energy and felt invincible. All of my senses were heightened and I knew with great certainty that I could save Ginny.

"Anxiety is toxic," he said. "Never let it rule you."

I wanted to kiss him, but settled for a much manlier bear hug. The unmistakable thunder of Harley Davidson motorcycles interrupted our embrace and we made our way back to the house.

Six hogs thundered toward us in a staggered formation. There wasn't a rice burner in the group. The lead chopper flew a black flag with a red dragon, its left claw squeezed blood from a beating heart and the right supported a big set of testicles. The dragon image was also inlaid into the chopper's paint job, flowing from the front fender to the rear. A small bell dangled from the bike's frame, just inches from the asphalt, as a warning to the road gremlins that they weren't to mess with this bike.

The solo saddle made it clear that this biker always road alone. The wide seat was filled with an even wider ass supporting a gut that hung way over the gas tank. The biker's belly was covered with a tattoo of the red dragon except its claws stretched from his chest down into his dirty jeans. Long greasy salt and pepper hair was pulled back into a French braid. Mr. Braid's long beard was divided into two similar braids that were tied off with chrome pony tail holders.

The next two bikes were less flashy...a couple of black Harley Low Riders with lots of chrome. The riders, however, were a different story. It was two chicks as different as night and day. The blond wore her hair man short and spiked at crazy angles. She wore no makeup and her only adornment was a hand full of huge silver rings that, when taken as a whole, formed the shape of a dragon. In fact, it looked like a set of fancy brass knuckles.

This chick looked like she could put a hurting on someone. Her thick muscular biceps would have made any body-builder proud. Obviously, she spent a lot of time in the gym. In fact, the closer I looked the more convinced I became she was a body builder herself. Ms. Amazon's shoulders, back, chest, and thighs were massive, like her biceps. She was a big girl, but there wasn't an ounce of fat on her. Odd, but she had this massive chest and no tits.

A thick black leather sweat band displayed a hot pink dragon centered on her forehead. Just below the dragon, wrap-around sun glasses rested on the bridge of her nose. Both nostrils were pierced with pink studs. A wife beater was stretched tight across her chest. It was stenciled with hot pink lettering that proclaimed: "I'm a Survivor Motherfucker." A Susan G. Komen pink ribbon made it clear she was a breast cancer survivor.

Her faded jeans were held up by a thick black leather belt with an antique silver dragon buckle. The jeans were ripped at both knees and mid-thigh on the left. Strapped to the right thigh was a black handled commando knife. Her wardrobe was completed with square-toed black engineer boots.

The other chick was hot in a scary kind of way, all dressed in black like Cat Woman. This one had no need to confirm she was female. In fact, she wasn't wearing a shirt. Her double D's just barely squeezed into a black leather vest that looked as if it could burst at any moment.

She wore tight-fitting black leather pants that displayed a prominent camel toe. If there was any doubt about her role, a black leather whip with multiple tails tucked into her thigh-high dominatrix boots, made it clear she was the one who dealt out the punishment.

Ms. Dom's witchy black hair blew wild in the wind and partially obscured her freakish white face. For an instant it formed a tai chi pattern that most people call the yin-yang symbol. She wore no eye protection, unless you want to count black makeup painted in a jagged pattern around her green eyes. If there was any warmth in her wide Cheshire cat smile, it was lost in blood red lips that stood out in sharp contrast to her pale face.

Close behind Ms. Dom was a gorilla clinging to a set of ape hangers. These are tall handlebars that extend above the biker's head, giving the impression that he is hanging from a tree. He was the only rider wearing a helmet...a simple black brain bucket with stickers pasted all over it. He was still too far away to read them, but the red dragon pasted on the forehead was unmistakable.

There was no hair showing below the tiny helmet except for a mustache and goatee, unless you want to count the bushy unibrow. His brow was pinched tight and both corners of his eyes were pierced. King Kong had a square face and no neck. A thick tuft of reddish hair pushed its way through the neck of his Harley Davidson t-shirt.

The next rider in line rode hands free. In fact, he was arched backwards over the rear wheel with his arms spread wide palms facing the sun. "Ole' George" was painted on the tank of his vintage Harley Davidson Pan Head.

Ole' George wore a crumpled black Fedora.

I don't have a clue how he kept it from blowing away. Maybe the hat was just too intimidated to cross him. His craggy face was cut with four parallel lines rising from the corners of his mouth…one set to his nostrils and the other to his cheek bones.

Despite the hot weather, his raw boned frame was covered with multiple layers of clothing. It was nothing fancy…a blue jean vest with club patches, flannel shirt open to the navel, and a black Grateful Dead t-shirt. I don't consider myself a Deadhead, but for some reason I instantly heard a few lines of their song "Built to Last" play in my head.

The final biker was Eve's husband, Gil. Shit. This time he brought his gang with him. The bikers pulled to a stop in front of the house and shut down their hogs. The rumble of Screaming Eagle pipes was replaced by engineer boots crunching loose gravel. They spread out like hunters driving their prey to the kill. A beat-down seemed imminent, but I refused to be cowed. Instead, I waited…relaxed and ready to fight, if necessary. It was the smallest of the bikers who broke the silence.

In a gravelly voice Ole' George said, "You the motherfucker that killed Tiny?"

CHAPTER 22

Dragon Gate Motorcycle Club was formed after World War II by a couple of fighter pilots. They were joined by other servicemen who got a taste of the world in their fight against the evil empire and still weren't ready to settle down. Like the cowboy migration in the 1800's, they mounted their iron horses and hit the trail. Their only goal was to explore the land of the free and home of the brave.

The club had its ups and downs over the years. In the 1960's an over-zealous prosecutor looking to advance his political career fabricated a case against one of their members. It resulted in a high profile prosecution that was, eventually, withdrawn for lack of evidence. It left a bitter taste in their mouths.

The incident also created a public perception that motorcycle clubs are infested with violent criminals. Hollywood made a few movies about bikers that reinforced the public perception that they are dangerous outlaws.

Of course, some bikers really are thugs who do nothing to dispel the outlaw myth. Instead, they use it to intimidate others and very few are willing to show them any disrespect. Of all the biker clubs, Dragon Gate had the worst reputation. The menacing group that now surrounded me certainly lived up to it.

The ragtag group of bikers standing in front of me thought that I had killed the president of their motorcycle club. If not handled well, somebody was going to get hurt, and it would likely be me.

Most martial arts make a show of being hard, strong, and fast. By contrast, Tai Chi is calm, centered, and peaceful. It is a mystery to most people how something so peaceful-looking can be used for self-defense purposes. Yet, in ancient China, it was revered as one of the most effective fighting styles. So what is the secret?

I first learned the secret of Tai Chi on my sixteenth birthday when Ch'ing tossed me the keys to his car and said, "Let's try out that new learner's permit."

I jumped at the opportunity to get a driving lesson. A license is everything to a teenage boy. Without one, dating is impossible.

Thinking we'd start slow, I asked, "Are we going to stay in the neighborhood?"

"Head to the Interstate," he answered.

I felt my stomach flop. I'm not sure what I expected, but Ch'ing told me to relax and not overreact.

"Just point it between the lines, Grant," said Ch'ing. "If you remember to make small adjustments, then you'll be okay."

Gulping, I backed down the driveway and did what he said. I figured he'd offer more driving instruction, but instead, he talked about his life in the monastery.

"Once a year, the old monks descend the mountain with food, wine, and medicine," Ch'ing said. "First, they tend to the sick. Afterwards, they throw a huge party for the villagers, entertaining them with stories and martial arts demonstrations."

"I wish I could watch them do Kung Fu," I said. "Ch'ing, what is the ultimate martial art?"

Without hesitation he answered, "Tai Chi."

"Yea, right," I said. "It's so slow. How could anyone fight with that stuff? I mean, it's for old men, isn't it?"

He didn't answer. Instead, he said we needed gas and told me to take the next exit. Ch'ing went inside to pay as I began pumping fuel into his old convertible Cadillac.

For the first time, I gave our surroundings a good look. It was a very rough area. The streets were empty. All the other businesses looked closed. Most of the buildings in the immediate area were boarded. Vacant structures were covered in gang graffiti. The convenience store windows were covered with bars. I realized this was a very scary place.

As I surveyed my surroundings, I saw something move in the shadows. I couldn't quite make it out at first. Slowly, a sinister figure emerged and took shape. His face was hidden by a hooded sweatshirt. He paused for what seemed like an eternity, and then began to move in my direction.

I did not like the looks of this at all. I felt my heart start pounding and I couldn't catch my breath. My blood pressure increased a notch with each menacing step. By the time he stopped a few feet in front of me, I was in a full blown fight or flight state.

Time slowed. Sweat trickled down the small of my back. He shifted his feet and mumbled something unintelligible. It was a strange garbled sound. I wasn't even sure it was speech. So much information can be gained about a person in just a few sentences. If you listen carefully, you can read their intentions. I learned nothing from the garbled sounds coming from him. I was frozen. I waited.

I tried to see his face…read his eyes and expression. Even at close range, his face was still obscured. He was like a shadow and it totally creeped me out. He spoke again. I still didn't understand him. This time I responded, but my voice cracked before coming out high and sharp. Damn, I didn't mean to do that.

He snorted in disgust and reached for his pocket. He was going for a weapon. My only chance was to hit him hard and fast. I was a split second away from attacking when I heard Ch'ing's warm friendly voice.

"What can we do for you friend?" asked Ch'ing.

Ch'ing had appeared out of nowhere. He quietly sided up to the stranger and put his arm around him. His manner was friendly. The embrace was warm. He used the connection to trap the mugger's arm against his body. The hand reaching for the weapon was immobilized in the thug's pocket. Ch'ing's smile never wavered. His kindness was genuine. His control of the situation was absolute.

The shadow turned to look at Ch'ing. For the first time, I could see the mugger's face. It quickly shifted from hatred to shock and confusion. Ch'ing's appearance had been so unexpected. His lighthearted and friendly demeanor was equally astonishing.

As I processed this unexpected turn of events, I witnessed the most amazing transformation. Slowly, the mugger's face changed until it mirrored Ch'ing's warmth and friendliness. He visibly relaxed. His eyes began to twinkle just like my teacher's. Ch'ing repeated his question. This time more softly.

"What can we do to help you friend?" asked Ch'ing.

After handing him a couple of cigarettes, Ch'ing gave him a pat on the back and sent him off into the night.

His parting words were, "Be careful my friend. It can be dangerous out there."

We climbed into the car and started for home. Neither of us spoke for a while. I was thinking about what could have happened and my hands started shaking.

I needed to talk about it so I asked Ch'ing, "What happened back there?"

"Tai Chi lesson," he answered.

"Lesson?" I asked.

"It's easy to hurt people," said Ch'ing. "That takes little skill. The greater skill is to diffuse aggression without causing harm. The best way to do that is to win the fight before it begins. Nip it in the bud, to quote your great American philosopher, Barney Fife."

"I don't understand," I said. "That wasn't a fight."

He looked at me and said softly, "Then, why are your hands still shaking."

I thought I had hidden it. I should have

known better. Ch'ing doesn't miss anything. I knew better than to give him a bullshit answer.

"I thought he was going to kill me," I said. "It scared me."

Ch'ing patted me on the shoulder.

"You did good," said Ch'ing. "You stood in the face of danger and didn't overreact."

More honesty from me.

"The truth is I was about to punch him when you appeared out of nowhere," I said.

"The better strategy is to embrace rather than destroy," replied Ch'ing.

"How do I do that?" I asked.

"Join energy at the onset of conflict," said Ch'ing.

"Huh?"

"Never run from conflict," said Ch'ing. "Enter a dangerous situation and lead the attacker to safety. That is true martial mastery. Anything else falls short of the objective of an enlightened master."

That's exactly what Ch'ing did. If I had not seen it for myself, I would have thought he was talking about an unrealistic philosophy.

"Can you teach me Tai Chi?" I asked.

"Tai Chi is for living," said Ch'ing. "It is about balance. The symbol people call the yin-yang symbol is a graphic representation of Tai Chi. It depicts opposites in balance. Opposites need each other. Light does not exist except in relationship to dark. Good and evil define one another. Grant, did you think that young man at the gas station was evil?"

"I thought he was bad guy," I confessed.

Ch'ing pressed, "Do you wish there was no bad in the world, Grant?"

I answered without thinking.

"Yes, I do," I said. "Then, we would have a perfect world, don't you think?"

Ch'ing shook his head.

"Good and bad define each other," said Ch'ing. "If bad ceases to exist, then, so does good. When good and bad are out of balance, our life is filled with turmoil. The goal is to embrace life as it is. It does no good wishing things were different. If you can manage this, then you will be able to smile in the face of danger."

I was brought back to the present by a low growl. Ole' George was waiting for an answer to his question. He thought I was Tiny's killer. As I looked into his eyes, I saw his pain. I know what it feels like to lose a loved one. I didn't know if he would believe me, but it was time to tell him what happened.

"I found Tiny in a pool of blood," I said. "I did everything I could to save him, but...I'm sorry you lost your friend, man."

Ole' George studied me long and hard before reaching around to his low back. Remembering Ch'ing's lesson, I resisted the temptation to spring for his throat. It was the right decision. Ole' George pulled out a bottle of bourbon, slowly opened it, took a long draw, and then, offered the whiskey to me.

Even though I had just had breakfast, it somehow seemed to fit the moment, so solemnly I took a drink. It was the strangest communion I ever shared.

Bourbon burns as it slides down the throat, but the whiskey he offered burns more softly than most. It is smooth, very smooth whiskey. Instead of fighting the burn, I embraced it and let it send my thoughts back to race days at the horse track with Dad.

He loved the track, but not because he was gambler. Dad loved the horses. For me, a day at the track was a day filled with the smell of bourbon, cigars, and horse manure. It was something we did together and bourbon always reminded me of those happy days.

After the burn subsided and I returned to the present moment, I handed the bottle back to Ole' George. Just when I thought the day couldn't get any weirder, my hand touched Ole George's and he said, "It's a good day to die."

And that's when the phone finally rang.

CHAPTER 23

Disrespecting a Dragon is never a good idea, but the most important thing at that moment was the phone call. Tiny was dead. Ginny might end up that way too, if I didn't take the call.

I looked at Ole' George and said, "I'm sorry your friend is dead, but I am taking this call. It's a matter of life or death."

As I dug a hand into my pocket, the biker scowled and spat an ugly green mess at my feet. That wasn't the reaction I hoped for, but now he was starting to piss me off.

"Someone I care about was abducted," I said. "I think it was Tiny's killer who took her."

I didn't wait for his permission. Instead, I answered the phone hoping to hear Ginny's voice. I was disappointed. It was the same voice that had forced its way onto the line earlier. Androgynous, is the best description of the voice I heard...not masculine or feminine...neutral.

"They're going to kill you, you know," said the caller.

"Maybe," I said.

"It would save me the trouble of doing it

myself, but I need to talk to you first."

"I'm not talking to you until I know Ginny is okay," I said.

"Patience grasshopper," said the caller.

"Do you still have Ginny?" I demanded.

"There's an abandoned warehouse on West Market near the Shawnee Expressway," said the voice. "Bring the monk and be there in an hour. If you're one minute late...she dies. If you call the police, she dies."

"If you hurt her, I will kill you," I said.

The caller paused.

"If you want this pretty little thing to live, find a way to stay alive," said the caller.

That was it. The call abruptly ended. Sometime during the brief call the Dragons had pulled weapons and moved a step closer. Ole' George was pointing a .44 Magnum at me. Why do the little guys always carry the biggest guns? It was almost as big as him. He was maybe 5'7" and couldn't have weighed more than 130 pounds, soaking wet.

Ms. Dom brandished the cat o' nines. The crack of her whip added a surreal sound to the scene. The Amazon held her knife commando-style. Mr. Braids was pointing a Glock at my chest. The tip of the barrel was all I could see of the gun in King Kong's massive hands.

I needed to convince them I wasn't Tiny's

killer, but, when I opened my mouth to speak, Ole' George shook his head and pulled the .44's hammer. That's when a red dot appeared on the first knuckle of his forefinger. Someone had him dead in his sights, and I knew that someone had to be Uncle Jim.

Ole' George saw it and muttered, "What the…"

The laser dot quickly moved to Ole' George's heart and, then, to his right eye. But, it didn't rest there. In a flash, it moved to King Kong's forehead and, then, to Amazon's chest. The red dot never stopped. It continued dancing from target to target.

"Uncle Jim was a marine sniper," I said casually. "If you lay down your weapons he might be willing to tell you about the time he snuck into Pakistan and singlehandedly took out an Al-Qaeda cell."

Surprisingly, it was Ms. Dom who showed the first signs of submission. I guess she figured a whip wasn't much use against a sniper rifle. Or maybe, she had a streak of sub deep inside of her that was dying to get out. Either way, Ole' George was having none of it.

He glared at me and said in a voice loud enough for Uncle Jim to hear, "Man, I ain't leaving nothing on the table. I'm gonna use every bit until there ain't nothing left of me. Not a damn thing for any of you fucking buzzards. One minute Ole' George will be here and then poof I'll be gone. That's cuz I'll be all used up. So, just try to shoot me motherfucker before I put a golf ball size hole in pretty boy's chest."

Let me tell you what folks...Ole' George is one crazy dude. I knew at that moment, beyond a shadow of a doubt, he was going to get a bunch of us killed.

Just when it seemed like my death was imminent, I was granted a reprieve. It was the sound of a Harley that provided a moment of respite. It's like biker catnip. They can't seem to get enough of it. No matter what they are doing, they pause and turn their attention toward an approaching bike.

Unlike the bikers, I never once took my eyes off Ole' George. Ch'ing had taught me well and I knew better than to let anything distract me from a threat. It wasn't until the rider pulled into my field of vision that I recognized the bike.

Eric is one of those guys who wear a smile like it's their favorite pair of jeans. Comfortable, may be the best way to describe it. He wasn't smiling as he backed the Road King next to the other motorcycles, dropped the kick stand and dismounted.

Ch'ing did his best to teach Eric that fighting is never the solution to a problem, but Eric loves a good fight. A few years ago, he was confronted by four muggers as he and Kinsey were leaving a bar. Eric grinned and said something to Kinsey about how much fun it was going to be. When she rolled her eyes and yawned, the muggers fled.

I figured this situation was going to escalate now that Eric was here, but he surprised me. Instead of displaying his usual macho attitude, he walked straight to Ole' George, placed himself between me and the gun, and gave him a warm hug.

Ole' George laid his head on Eric's chest and began crying. At first it was just a tear slipping down his cheek, but then it turned to sobs. Eric didn't say a word. He just held him.

When Ole' George was cried out, Eric finally said, "I can't imagine the pain of losing the love of your life, my friend."

That started another round of tears. Not just for Ole' George, but all of the biker's had tears in their eyes. It only lasted a minute or so before King Kong realized he was crying in front of strangers. Looking thoroughly embarrassed, he wiped his eyes with the back of his gun hand and pulled himself together. One by one the others did the same.

"You all need to put your weapons away," said Eric.

Ole' George nodded and slipped the Dirty

Harry cannon into his waistband. I've never understood why someone would want to point the barrel of a gun toward their junk. The rest of the bikers followed his lead and stashed their weapons in various nooks and crannies.

"Tell me, my friend, why you were pointing that cannon at Grant," said Eric.

"A friend on the force told me his prints were on the murder weapon, his and some chick's," said Ole' George.

The Amazon jabbed her thumb at me and said, "He doesn't think a chick could ever take Tiny out, so, it had to be him. Especially, since he was trained by the same guy who taught you to fight."

"The chick's name is Kim Slotter," I said. "She's ex-special forces and a serious bad-ass."

I pulled up my shirt and pointed to the knife wound. "It's just a scratch, but she cut me when I found her in Tiny's office," I said. "Same with the bullet wound next to it. There was a shooting at the Center and I caught a bullet."

"Show them the truck," said Uncle Jim.

I had no idea Uncle Jim was right behind me. For a guy with a cane, he can move like a cat when he needs to. The truck had been parked on the street in front of my apartment when the swat team arrested me, but there it sat in the driveway. The back glass was shattered and the tail gate sported three bullet holes.

"There was a second shooting in the parking garage at the Center," I said.

Nodding in Padma's direction, I continued, "Somebody wants us dead. It's starting to look like they may have hired Slotter to do the job. Ginny was kidnapped and they are holding her hostage at a warehouse out by the Shawnee Parkway. If Padma and I don't get there soon, they are going to kill Ginny."

Gil spoke up for the first time and asked, "Is she the one who gave me the ring and then walked out on you?"

"Yes, that's her," I answered.

"I like her and am not going to let someone hurt her," said Gil. "She may have just saved your life. Let him go, George."

Ole' George nodded.

"Okay, but Slotter is mine," said Ole' George. "I'll show the bitch what a bad ass is."

I pulled Eric aside and said, "This guy is a loose cannon. He could get Ginny killed."

"I know Grant, but you'll never convince him to stay behind," said Eric. "Let's find a way to make him an asset."

"I got a bad feeling about this, Eric," I said.

"Ah, don't sweat it man," said Eric. "It'll be fun. So, what's the plan, buddy?"

I didn't have a plan, so, what I said was,

"We're going to do whatever it takes to rescue Ginny."

Eric grinned at me and said, "I like it."

"We could use the bikers as a diversion," I said.

"Now we're getting somewhere," said Eric. "While the bad guys focus on the bikers, Uncle Jim can position himself at a strategic location with his sniper rifle."

"Time is not on our side right now," said Uncle Jim. "It's time to move out. Grant, I need to speak with you for a minute before we leave?"

As the bikers rode off in a thunder with Eric trailing them, Uncle Jim pulled me aside.

Looking a little uncomfortable, he said, "I just wanted to say, I love you, son. Be safe."

This was so unexpected. I know he loves me, but he's never actually said it. I was choked up and tried to respond, but he waved it off as he walked away.

I was still recovering from the shock as Uncle Jim backed his classic 1963 Corvette Sting Ray out of the garage. It's the model with the split rear window and it's in pristine condition. He had it painted a beautiful candy apple red and usually only takes it out for an occasional Sunday drive or other special occasions. I guess he figured this was a special occasion.

Padma's eyes bugged out of his head when he

saw the car.

Uncle Jim smiled and asked, "Padma, do you want to ride with me?"

"Slotter is expecting me and Padma," I said. "He has to ride with me."

It might be the only time I've seen Padma show disappointment as Bird hopped from his shoulder and took his spot in the passenger seat. That surprised all of us, and I think Uncle Jim was about to tell him to get out of his car when Bird glared at him. Bird's glare is not something you take lightly and Uncle Jim knew it. So he shrugged, fired up the 360 horse power V-8 and followed the bikes out of the neighborhood.

Time was running out on Ginny. Padma and I hurried to the truck, but when I turned the key, nothing happened. I tried again and still nothing. The truck was dead in the water. Shit, we had no way to get there.

CHAPTER 24

Dad's truck was dead. If I didn't get us to the warehouse soon, Ginny would be too. I couldn't believe it. The old rust bucket wasn't pretty, but had always been reliable. Eric thought I was crazy, but I had trusted it during my travels across the country. Not once had it ever let me down. The last road trip was to Glacier National Park for a backpacking trip a few weeks earlier.

"That does not sound good, Master Li," said Padma in his ridiculously cheerful voice.

If I hadn't been in shock about the truck and filled with worry about Ginny's safety, I might have taken a moment to wonder why he called me that, but I was too busy feeling tested like the biblical Job. How many setbacks can a man endure before he loses faith in himself? I guess that's the question we all have to answer for ourselves.

"Focus on the challenge before you," said Padma. "What's the solution?"

The truck needed repairs, but there wasn't time. We were at the end of the sidewalk and needed to leave immediately. I knew what I had to do. My mind was racing for some other option, and there was one, but it was the last thing I wanted to do. On the verge of panic, an image of Ginny popped into my mind. I pictured her scared and hurt. I had made my decision.

"Come with me," I said.

We hurried to the back of the house and stood in front of the garage. Taking a deep breath, I raised the overhead door. The inside was neat and orderly. This was Uncle Jim's man cave and he ran a tight ship. Everything had its place.

In the corner, hidden by an old bed sheet covered with faded yellow daisies, was the thing I hated most in this world. Padma patted me on the shoulder and gave me a little nudge in its direction. I wasn't sure I could do this.

My feet didn't want to move, but I willed myself forward until we stood next to it. I could feel the blood pounding in my temples as I reached for the sheet and tossed it to the floor. There she was. For the first time in years, I looked at the motorcycle that had killed Dad.

Glancing at my clenched fists, Padma said, "You look like you want to hurt someone."

I relaxed my hands and answered in a hoarse whisper, "This was Dad's bike."

Padma eyed the bike.

"It is pristine," he said.

I choked. The damn thing took my parents

from me and it didn't have a scratch on it. They were thrown head-first into a culvert. The bike landed in a pile of leaves.

"After the funeral, Uncle Jim rolled it into this corner," I said. "It hasn't been moved since. Ch'ing brought me in here once. We silently stood in this very spot for a long while…just looking. After I cried myself out, he patted me on the shoulder and told me this magnificent machine would save me some day. I can't imagine how. I hate this bike."

"Love and hate are opposite sides of the same coin," said Padma.

Maybe Ch'ing was right, after all. The thing I hated most in the world would carry me back to something that had been missing for many years in my life…love. After all these years, I realized I still loved the little girl who had now grown into a beautiful woman.

Resigned, I swung my leg over the saddle and settled in. Surprisingly, it felt comfortable. It was a big bike and I expected it to be heavy and clumsy. It wasn't. Instead, it was beautifully balanced.

"Let's see if she'll start after all these years," I said.

Taking a deep breath, I hit the starter. The engine churned without firing. I lifted my thumb from the start button.

"Damn," I muttered under my breath.

Padma patted me on the shoulder and said, "Try again."

This was my chance to redeem myself...to heal old wounds left festering too long. I wasn't about to let Ginny down...again. I wanted redemption. Failure was not an option.

My determination calmed me and, for some reason, I knew the bike would start. The engine fired on the next try. The rumble of the old Harley's pipes was like a victory shout.

I grinned at Padma and said, "Climb on. We can still make it to the warehouse in time if we hurry. Let's find out what this bitch wants with us and get Ginny home safely."

Padma didn't hesitate. He hiked up his robe, swung his leg over the back and settled in behind me. It was kind of weird having him back there, but I tried not to think about it too much. Instead, I focused on backing the hog out of the garage and off we rode to rescue Ginny.

It's a twenty minute drive across town from the east end to the west end and we had eighteen minutes to get there. It was no time to worry about a speeding ticket, but a traffic stop would be disastrous. We had no time to spare and the risk was necessary. I trusted my instincts to slow down, if necessary. So, we flew down I-71 toward the west end, like a bat out of hell.

The west end's ghettos are the source of Louisville's reputation as one of the most dangerous places in the country to live. Like most ghettos, there isn't much of a police presence. The natives are left to fend for themselves and extreme poverty brings out the worst in people.

The area is near a port that services barges running up and down the Ohio River between the steel mills of the northeast and the Gulf of Mexico to the southwest. As a result of the fading steel industry and the general economic downturn in this area, many of the warehouses are empty. Finding a particular warehouse might not be easy.

It was Padma who solved the problem. He pointed toward a huge building with decayed red brick. Faded paint announced it was once the home of the best damn bourbon in Kentucky. It had a few broken windows and rust was overtaking the paint. Someone had cut the chain lock and the entry gate was standing open.

Weeds pushed through the cracked asphalt parking lot. I maneuvered the bike around the potholes and loose gravel. The lot was empty, so we circled around to the back.

It's hard to believe, but the rear of the building was in worse shape than the front. Chunks of brick had crumbled from the façade and lay in pieces among the weeds. What was left of the wall was covered in gang graffiti. A rusted eight foot chain link fence with razor wire at the top ran the property line. Someone had pulled it open in several places to gain access to the property.

A black SUV was parked next to the loading docks. Uncle Jim and the Dragons were nowhere in sight. I rolled to a stop about twenty yards from the SUV and killed the engine. Tinted windows hid the driver from view. There wasn't any sound except a creaking door and the occasional rustle of leaves in the undergrowth along the fence line. Someone had written "ENDGAME" on the door using firehouse red spray paint.

I dropped the kickstand and we dismounted. Three of the SUV's doors opened, but no one got out. There was nothing to do but wait.

Finally, after what seemed like an eternity, three men climbed out of the SUV and headed in our direction. Ginny was not with them. The driver was a big man with a thick neck, barrel chest, and huge muscular arms. Shrek was wearing camouflage pants, a wife beater, and combat boots. His head was shaved and every inch of visible skin was covered in strange tattoos.

The man who'd been riding shotgun was much

smaller with cold eyes and a hard face filled with contempt. He was hairy. His unruly black hair hung low on his forehead like a sheep dog. He wore faded jeans and a Hawaiian shirt opened at the neck exposing a big tuft of curly black hair. Bizarrely, Mr. Hawaiian Tropic's white sneakers looked like they were fresh out of the box.

The third man had an ugly, jagged scar running from the corner of the mouth to his ear lobe. Scarface was wearing black jeans, black polo shirt, and black combat boots. He was about six feet tall with a tight, compact frame. His hair was cut in a 1950's flat-top style. There was an airborne symbol tattooed onto his muscular forearm.

They stopped about three paces in front of us and spread out. Scarface was in the center. Mr. Hawaiian Tropic was to his right and Shrek took up position on the other side. Mr. Hawaiian Tropic leered at Padma. Shrek's jaw twitched. Scarface tried to stare me down. I resisted the temptation to break the silence and waited for him to speak first.

It took a couple of minutes before Scarface finally asked, "You come alone?"

I nodded in Padma's direction and asked, "Where's Ginny?"

I was starting to think that Scarface wasn't going to respond, but then, he raised his hand

and motioned someone in the SUV to come forward. The fourth door opened and two women climbed out.

Ginny was gagged with a red ball connected to a black leather strap that was secured at the back of her head. Her hands were tied in front with white plastic zip ties. There was a trickle of blood from a cut somewhere above the hairline. I noticed a tear in her dress. She was subdued...maybe in shock.

I knew these guys played rough and I couldn't believe I had left my gun under the seat of the truck. There's nothing like bringing your fists to a gun fight. The odds were not good, but thankfully, Ch'ing had trained me well. I set my jaw in anticipation of the fight to come.

When I noticed the deference Scarface gave the woman standing next to Ginny, I took a closer look. The hair was longer and the clothes were more feminine, but it was Slotter. No question about it.

"Your Harley is an old man's bike," said Slotter. "I prefer my Ducati."

I suddenly felt the need to defend Dad's bike, but resisted because I knew that Slotter was obviously baiting me. She wanted to know if I could be easily provoked into an emotional outburst. One of the keys to a successful negotiation is patience. I waited to see if she would need to fill the silence. She did.

"That's an antique," she said. "A mint condition Heritage Classic Softail. Doesn't look like it has been ridden much. Are you an owner instead of a rider?"

I didn't answer, so she said, "You are one of those pussies who always plays it safe…watching from a safe distance while other people live their lives. I bet you'd enjoy watching me do your girlfriend while you two-finger that little wanger of yours. What do you say to a little girl-on-girl action?"

She cut her eyes to Padma and said, "You probably prefer the company of men. Is this teddy bear your biker bitch?"

Ginny crinkled her nose like she had just stepped into a construction crew's port-of-potty on a hot summer day. I wasn't sure if it was the idea of being raped by Slotter or the thought of seeing me with another man. But, I was glad she was showing signs of life.

We needed to get off this subject, so I finally spoke, "Did you go to all this trouble getting us here just to taunt us?"

"Glad to hear you're not a mute too," said Slotter.

From the corner of my eye, I caught a glimpse of movement on the warehouse rooftop. Hopefully, it was Uncle Jim and not one of

Slotter's men.

"You got what you wanted," I said. "Let her go."

"Actually, I wanted all three of you here," said Slotter. "So thanks for cooperating and bringing me the monk."

I had no idea why she wanted all three of us. Sooner or later I knew she would get to the point, so I waited.

"Where is he, Padma," she asked.

Padma seemed to understand but, didn't answer Slotter.

"Who are you talking about?" I asked.

Slotter nodded toward Ginny.

"Why Barbie Doll's father of course."

CHAPTER 25

We are born into violence. Like a newborn forced from the womb and slapped on the ass, Ginny let loose a muffled wail that even the ball gag couldn't entirely suppress. Since she couldn't ask the question, I asked it for her.

"Is Ginny's father alive?" I asked.

That's pretty much when all hell broke loose. The Dragons stormed around the corner of the building, but it was nothing like a cavalry charge. Instead of a tight military formation, they were weaving in and out like amusement park bumper cars. I couldn't make much sense of the keystone cop strategy until the bikers suddenly scattered and came at us from multiple directions. They were trying to surround Slotter.

This was going to end badly and I wanted to get Ginny out of the line of fire. Slotter's men froze and nervously tracked the bikers' movements. I looked for a chance to rescue her. It wasn't going to be easy. Slotter's grip tightened on Ginny's upper arm and the barrel of her gun was pointed at my chest.

"You'll be the first one to die, pretty boy,"

shouted Slotter. "Wave 'em off."

"This isn't my doing," I said. "They're acting on their own and you brought this on yourself when you killed Tiny."

She was only confused for a moment before saying, "You must mean the fat-ass security guard at the Center."

I nodded.

"He was their president," I said.

"That wasn't me," she said with a shrug and a smirk.

"Right," I said.

"I guess that makes you the low hanging fruit," she said. "You're the easiest problem to deal with, so I might as well kill you now."

Suddenly, gunfire flashed from the rooftop and Slotter's weapon clattered to the ground. She had been well-trained. Instead of confusion, she reacted immediately by turning toward the rooftop and pulling Ginny in front of her to serve as a human shield. She pulled another gun from her waistband and jammed the barrel into Ginny's ear.

"Show yourself or I blow her brains out," shouted Slotter.

A man rose near the roof's edge. I expected to see Uncle Jim with his hands in the air, but instead of an eye patch I saw a long blond ponytail hanging midway down the back of a Bob

Marley t-shirt. Geez it was Pony Tail. This guy seems to be everywhere.

"Both of you," demanded Slotter.

Uncle Jim slowly stood up next to Pony Tail. His sniper rifle was held high above his head. He looked thoroughly disgusted with himself.

"Toss the rifle," said Slotter.

Uncle Jim complied with Slotter's demand and threw his gun over the side of the building. As the rifle fell toward the ground, Slotter swept her gun toward Uncle Jim and was taking aim when a flash of color streaked past.

Bird gave no advance warning unless you want to count a squawk about death from above as he slashed the back of Slotter's head. She let go of Ginny while she desperately tried to snatch Bird out of the air.

That was the opening I was waiting for, but Scarface moved a split-second before me. I thought he was going to block my path to Slotter, but instead he grabbed Bird and began shaking him.

"Aaawk, do I look like shake n' bake to you," screamed Bird.

Scarface stopped shaking for a moment and looked at Bird like he was some kind of alien. Then, he grabbed Bird's head with one hand and his body with the other as if he was going to wring his neck. I wouldn't have believed Padma could move that swiftly, but in the blink of an eye, he closed the gap between them and did some weird two finger typewriting thing over Scarface's body.

The thug appeared more annoyed than concerned by Padma's martial display. He snorted and rolled his eyes just before his limbs began shaking. The shakes only lasted a moment before his eyes rolled completely back, displaying nothing but white.

Scarface was a big man, but it seemed like the life had been sucked out him. He shrunk a size or two before collapsing in on himself and slowly crumbling to the ground. His death grip on Bird held and the foul mouth macaw disappeared somewhere under Scarface's massive body. I knew Bird could not possibly have survived that.

Slotter shrieked like a girl when Scarface collapsed. She swung her shooting hand in Padma's direction and would have blown a hole in his chest, but Ms. Dom caught her forearm with the whip and gave it a yank as she rode past her.

If it were anybody but Slotter, she would have been pulled to the ground and drug behind the bike like a bunch of wedding day tin cans. Her gun clattered to the ground, but Slotter managed to coil her arm around the whip a few rounds and give a yank. The Harley wobbled and changed course.

Ms. Dom tumbled from the wayward Harley just before it crashed into the side of the warehouse and exploded into flames. Amazon Chick broke rank and rushed to the aid of Ms. Dom, who lay in a crumbled heap of leather on the broken asphalt. The flames from the burning bike reached the building and it lit up like a match. Uncle Jim would soon be engulfed in flames.

Ginny took advantage of the distraction by inching back and creating space between her and Slotter. I had been so focused on Slotter that I didn't notice the bikers had closed ranks and dismounted.

I wanted to put more distance between the two groups and Ole' George provided the means when he reached for his gun. Somehow he managed to dislodge the bottle of bourbon and it shattered at his feet. That's when all the shooting really got started.

There's nothing like the sound of gunfire to make a man painfully aware that he isn't carrying a firearm. I'd like to tell you it makes me a bigger man than the bad guys with guns, but it just made me feel stupid and vulnerable.

While my attention was on the blazing building, Slotter must have scooped her gun up because, once again, it was pointing at my chest.

I knew I was about to die. I watched helplessly as her trigger finger squeezed. Time slowed. I saw the bullet leave the gun barrel. It would have killed me, but Ginny dove into its path and took the bullet intended for me.

Maybe it was rage or maybe I had nothing left to lose. Either way, something shifted inside me. The space between seeing what needed to be done and taking action disappeared. While Slotter stood in shock, I closed the gap between us and disarmed her with the simplest of moves. In one continuous action the gun was out of her hand and in mine. I wasted no time in pointing it at her face and would have pulled the trigger, but I was knocked to the ground.

I fell facing Ginny. She lay in a puddle of blood a few feet from me. Her eyes were closed, and I saw no signs of respiration. She was pale, very pale. I stretched a bloody hand in her direction, but she was just out of my reach. I wanted to get up and go to her, but there was a disconnection between thought and action.

I felt tired and was about to close my eyes when I heard sirens. I can't be sure, but I may have heard a scream come from the burning building. The sounds seemed so far away.

Faint red and blue shadows told me fire and police were already here. Rose was the first officer I saw. She was rushing in our direction. I was thinking how glad I was she would be the one to help Ginny, when I noticed her lips were moving. She was speaking but I couldn't quite make out the words, so I focused as hard as I could to read her lips.

I can't be sure, but it looked like she was saying, "You fucking bitch, you killed my daughter."

That's when I saw the gun in her hand...the one she shoved into Slotter's belly before pulling the trigger. As Slotter sunk to her knees, other uniformed policemen rushed in and disarmed Rose. They were gentle with her and held her as she quietly sobbed.

The last thing I saw before everything went black was Mr. Medals. He intercepted Slotter's gurney just before it reached an ambulance. Words were spoken. He flashed some sort of identification to the medics and then soldiers loaded Slotter onto a military helicopter.

I came to in a hospital room. A flat panel television hanging on the wall was tuned to CNN. The sound was turned down, but I could see a graphic reporting a tragedy in Kentucky. It said a gas leak killed 3,212 people gathered to hear Padma Ganesha speak about the happiest place on Earth.

A toilet flushed and Eric walked out of the bathroom. All of the events of the last few days came flooding back to me. I was overwhelmed with anger and sadness. Ginny, Uncle Jim, Bird, all gone.

"Hey buddy," said Eric. "I knew it would take more than a bullet in the back to keep you down."

I nodded toward the television and said, "That's not what happened."

The smile left Eric's face and was replaced with a pinched brow. He opened his mouth to speak, but then changed his mind and bit his lip instead. It wasn't like Eric to not speak his mind, but what was there to say. My whole world had been turned upside down in one fell-swoop and I had no idea why.

"Grant, we've all been so worried about you," said Eric.

In that moment, I made up my mind that someone would pay for my loss, but that's not what I said to Eric.

"I'll be fine," I said.

"That's the spirit," said Eric.

"We need to find out why they took Slotter," I said. "I'm sure it's connected to the mass murder at the Center."

Eric sat in the side chair and began rubbing his hands up and down his pant legs. He stood up and glanced around the room, without focusing on anything in particular, before looking at me and sitting down again.

I knew I had been shot and only God knows what pain medicine was coursing through my body, but Eric sure was acting weird. Then it hit me. I hadn't seen him at the warehouse when all the shooting was going on.

"I needed your help during this fight, where were you?" I asked.

He sat there for the longest time without answering.

Finally, he said, "She's upstairs in ICU."

"Really...that's a shock," I said. "I thought I saw them whisk her away to some secret location. I need to see her Eric. Get me up there."

"There's someone you need to see first," said Eric. "I'll be right back."

"Is it Uncle Jim?" I asked. "Is Bird with him?"

"I'm sorry," said Eric as he stepped out the door.

I felt myself deflate again. They were gone. Slotter had taken everything from me. They were all dead...every one of them. There was nothing left for me. I was all alone again, just like I'd always feared. Well, I was tired of coping with loss. I was going to do something about this. I needed to get upstairs and wasn't about to wait on Eric. Slotter was going to pay now.

I pulled the IV from my arm and rolled sideways enough to get my feet on the floor. The last thing I remember thinking was that the A/C must be broken.

I heard a familiar voice, but couldn't quite place it. It was hard work, but I managed to open my eyes. The face finally connected to the voice. It was Professor Filmore, my attorney.

"He's finally awake," said Filmore.

I heard a second voice, less familiar. It took a moment, but I finally connected it to Mr. Medals.

"You need to make him understand," said Mr. Medals. "If not then…"

Filmore made a small cutting motion with his hand that stopped Mr. Medals from finishing his sentence. I didn't like the implicit threat in Mr. Medals' voice. I figured he wanted to protect Slotter, and if I didn't cooperate with Mr. Medals, then what? I wanted to keep things light, but my voice was little higher than normal when I spoke.

"Got myself shot, Admiral," I said.

He managed a half-hearted smile that wasn't consistent with the shake of his head. It was odd. I couldn't imagine Filmore displaying such openly conflicted body language.

"This is a tough situation you're in," said the Admiral.

I don't know about you, but that's not what I wanted to hear from my attorney. He should have told me that he had worked his legal magic and that I could rest easy. Besides, why was he with the Mr. Medals? I did not like it one bit.

"Have you cleared me of the charges?" I asked.

"That depends on you," said Filmore.

"Either the charges are dropped, or not," I said. "Which is it?"

"The gas leak explanation for what occurred at the Center is necessary for national security," said Filmore. "There are nuances to this cover story that protect you. Without it, you will be the prime suspect for Tiny's murder and for the murders of everyone at the Center."

"What about Slotter," I asked.

"She plays a vital role in our plans for national security," said Mr. Medals. "You do not."

I knew I was screwed if I openly opposed them, so I said, "I understand."

Filmore raised an eyebrow, but said nothing. He motioned Mr. Medals toward the door and led him out of the room. I waited a few minutes for them to clear the area and, then, swung my feet to the floor. This time I would hold it together long-enough to repay Slotter for what she did to me.

I blocked the pain. I blocked everything that stood in my way. My sole focus was on taking one step at a time. Little by little, step by step, I made my way down the hall to the elevator and to the intensive care unit.

Once I reached ICU, I assumed she would be protected in a guarded room, but saw no guards. My next thought was they may be in the room with her, so I cautiously stuck my head in a few doors, but none of them was Slotter's room. I was beginning to doubt I'd find her, but continued looking.

Finally, I saw a nurse dressed in blue scrubs hovering over a patient who might be her. I was about to duck around the corner and wait for the nurse to leave when I noticed he was wearing sandals. There was something familiar about those sandals, and while I searched my memory, I let my eyes drift over the rest of the nurse's body. The blond ponytail gave him away.

I should have kept my mouth shut. What did I care if Pony Tail wanted revenge against Slotter. I couldn't, of course. Such was the pain of my loss.

"Take your hands off her," I said. "She's mine."

When he turned to face me, I think what surprised me the most was how open Pony Tail seemed. There was nothing adversarial about him. He wasn't guarded. He didn't look like he was buried under the weight of many secrets. He seemed authentic. His smile was real. Go figure.

Pony Tail took a step to the side, and with a graceful sweep of the arm, invited me to claim my prize.   A part of me wanted to remain cautious, to expect some kind of trick, but I didn't listen to that voice.   If I had, who knows what dark turn the moment might have taken. Instead, my feet led me to Ginny's side.   Her cheeks were rosy.   Her chest rose and fell with a strong breath.   And then her eyes opened.

# # #

Thank you for reading my book. Won't you please take a moment to leave a book review?

Peace out,
Robert

COMING SOON!

GREAT MOTHER

CONTINUE THE ADVENTURE

We hope you enjoyed reading *Naked Tao*. Read Robert's other books, *Nostrum Conspiracy* and *UnderBelly*. Soon to be released is Robert's fourth book, *Great Mother*.

What Others are Saying About *Nostrum Conspiracy*:

"Robert Grant is a master story teller...combines nonstop action with a touch of Far Eastern mysticism..." M. Wexler

"You've written something special..." D. Bruner.

We have included a sample chapter on the following pages for your enjoyment.

Excerpt from

NOSTRUM CONSPIRACY

CHAPTER 1

An instant turns into the tragedy of a lifetime when a bullet tears a pinky sized hole into the forehead of the woman you love. It is especially painful when you've spent a lifetime ignoring her.

I allowed a single tear to follow the path of least resistance to the corner of my mouth, before wiping it with the tip of the tongue. Savoring the slight burn from the salt, I tried to remember the last time I wept. No luck there. I'm sure I've cried before. A man would have to be emotionally bankrupt to have never cried.

I've been such a jerk, but there's one thing I know for sure, this is the first time I've shed a tear of joy. Ginny is alive. I don't know how, but she is alive. Somehow she survived the gun shot and still looks radiant. By comparison, I feel like I've been kicked by an ornery mule.

Ginny doesn't need the clothes her company designs to make her beautiful. Even in a flimsy hospital gown, she is stunning. Tall and athletic, her flawless legs led the eye upward toward a tight little behind, while waves of soft dark brown hair fell gracefully onto her broad swimmer's shoulders spotted with a few freckles despite her olive skin tone.

Her eyes sparkle with life. Even though I've known her as long as I can remember, I find their color difficult to pinpoint. It is an unusual shade of blue or green that is best described as the color of a tropical sea.

The rest of Ginny's face is equally magnificent. She has an aristocratic high bridged nose set between wide cheekbones that narrow into a high forehead. It is a beautiful face that is enhanced with the flush of radiant good health. You might even say all true beauty is a reflection of good health.

As happy as I was to see her like this, I thought I might be hallucinating. The last time I saw her she was lying in a pool of her own blood, pale and lifeless. Yet now I find her in a hospital bed, the model of good health. How the hell is that possible?

"You're alive," said Ginny.

I shook my head as if that would wipe away any illusions. Still, there was no mistaking her musical voice. It was time to test the waters.

"You died," I murmured.

"I knew Slotter was going to pull the trigger before she did," said Ginny. "Everything happened so slowly. When the hammer fell I only had one thought...deflect that bullet. I knew, without a doubt, I could do it...but I failed."

Kim Slotter was a war hero gone bad. She had kidnapped Ginny and held her at an abandoned warehouse in the wrong end of town. I took a ragtag group and tried to rescue her, but the heroic deed went south and we were shot by the bad guys.

"You succeeded in deflecting the bullet, but that shot was intended for me, not you," I said.

Ginny absentmindedly massaged the spot just above her heart. Without thinking I mirrored her movement and felt the bandages covering the exit wound. I was lucky. If the bullet had been slightly lower it would have killed me.

"You're wounded," she said. "I failed."

She thought only of protecting me and damn near got herself killed doing it. Without thinking, I gathered her into my arms and held her tight.

I had never done anything so rash in my life and had a moment where I thought maybe I had overstepped a boundary between us. The moment of doubt passed when Ginny melted into me like she had been there a thousand times before.

"You did not fail," I said. "It wasn't Slotter who did this to me. I was shot in the back by one of her minions."

The brush with death opened my eyes to a few things. Introspection has an annoying way of doing that. The thing that hurt the most as we lay together in an expanding puddle of blood was the regret.

I couldn't understand why I had ignored Ginny all of those years. None of the reasons that once seemed adequate withstood the test of final judgment as we faced death together.

After the wave of grief passed, I wiped the tears from her shoulder and reminded myself that somehow she was miraculously alive and well. The grief was replaced with self-doubt. She couldn't still be alive. I must be dreaming, or worse, experiencing a psychotic break.

Neither was acceptable and I was thinking of giving myself a good hard pinch, when our tender moment was interrupted by a disapproving voice.

"What do you think you're doing?"

A young nurse with a fake smile plastered across her face stormed into the room. Her dirty blond hair had been hastily smoothed back, leaving a few stubborn strands that refused to comply. Instead, they curled around a flushed cheek, as testament to her refusal to follow the straight and narrow. On the opposite side of her face, a streak of dark mascara ran a quarter-inch from the corner of her left eye.

She was dressed in rumpled surgical scrubs

and the buttons on her top were out of alignment. She smelled of sweat from a quick tryst in some dark corner of the hospital.

Her name tag identified her as Nurse Nightshade. She was trying hard to be perky, but failed miserably. I had the sense Nurse Nightshade was trained to be upbeat, but it didn't come naturally to her. It was obvious she wasn't pleased with me.

"This patient is in critical condition," she said coldly. "I'm going to change her bandage and afterwards you need to leave so she can get some rest."

For someone charged with patient care, she was shockingly unobservant. She hadn't once looked at Ginny and seemed content to glare at me instead.

I nodded toward Ginny. Nurse Nightshade followed my eyes. At first she didn't seem to register what was in front of her, but when it finally sunk in that Ginny was the model of good health, she muffled a small scream with her hand.

"That's impossible," gasped Nurse Nightshade. "She's at death's door and Doctor Wiemp doesn't expect her to make it through the night."

It irked me that she gave more weight to what the Doctor said than what her own eyes revealed about Ginny's condition. Clearly, she was not at death's door. Ginny was alive and well.

I wanted to point this out to her, but resisted the temptation.

Instead I asked, "How do you explain it then…a miracle maybe?"

Nurse Nightshade ignored my question. Instead she made the sign of the cross, as if that would somehow protect her from something she didn't understand. I can't be certain, but I think I also heard her whisper something about God's own miracle.

I wasn't serious about the miracle comment, but that didn't seem to matter much to her. Once she completed the religious rituals, her nurses' training took over and she busied herself with Ginny's bandage.

At first she seemed hesitant, as if she feared what lay beneath it. Her fear didn't last long before she made up her mind to do her job and began to slowly remove the blood crusted dressing.

While she fussed with the bandage, I turned to ask Pony Tail what he knew about Ginny's condition, but he was nowhere in sight. Weird, I thought. He had been dressed in nurse's scrubs and hovering over Ginny when I walked into the room a few minutes earlier. I sure didn't hear him leave.

"Maybe the other nurse knows what happened to Ginny," I said to Nurse Nightshade.

Her attention was on the bandage and I wasn't sure if she heard me at first. I was about to repeat it when she finally answered.

"I'm the only one working this shift," she said.

"There was a male nurse in here a few minutes ago," I said.

Since she ignored me, I added a description of Pony Tail to give her memory a boost.

"He's in his mid-twenties, medium height, brown skin, and blond hair," I said.

I still didn't get a response from her, so I lamely continued with the description in the hopes something would register with her.

"He wears his hair long, but tied back in a ponytail," I said. "You can't miss him."

Nurse Nightshade was rude, but she was also working so I didn't take it personally. Besides, her focus was on carefully removing Ginny's bandages and I didn't want to distract her. It almost felt random when she finally responded with a shake of her head.

"There's no one like that here," she said.

I gave up on Pony Tail and chalked it up as one more strange mystery to follow-up at a later time.

While the nurse fussed with the bandages I

took a moment to look around the room. Hospital rooms are places where I put on horse blinders, since it's best not to see too much. The rooms tend to be stark and filled with unpleasant odors. For the most part, Ginny's room was no exception. However, it did have one interesting feature that drew my eye.

An odd picture hung on the wall next to the bathroom. Most art work in hospital rooms is virtually invisible, but this one caught my eye. It was a wreath, but I saw something odd hidden in its design. I could very clearly see a snake eating a bird. It appeared to be the same symbol vandals painted on Ch'ing's wall.

Ch'ing is my martial arts teacher who mysteriously disappeared a few days ago. When we searched his house for him, we found it had been vandalized. For some unknown reason, they had spray painted the snake eating bird symbol on the wall along with the message, "It has begun."

Nurse Nightshade removed the last of the bandages and gasped. Since she was obstructing my view, I craned my neck to see around her, but still couldn't see a thing.

I wasn't sure what to expect. I know I saw Slotter blow a hole in her forehead and a sick part of me wanted that hole to be there, so I wouldn't have to face the possibility I was crazy.

The rest of me wanted Ginny's forehead to be as smooth as a baby's butt.

When Nurse Nightshade finally shifted positions, what I saw was a bit of dried blood that she wiped away. Where there was once a hole the size of my little finger, now there was only smooth healthy skin. There was no evidence Ginny had suffered an injury.

I was relieved for sure, but now I doubted my memory of the events at the warehouse. Was Ginny really taken by an ex-special forces renegade and held hostage in a warehouse in West Louisville?

A group of us went to rescue her, but all hell broke loose. I was shot. Ginny was shot. The only family I had left was trapped on the roof of a burning building. I don't know how Uncle Jim could have survived those flames. Oh…and my crazy macaw, Bird, went down underneath a tank of a man.

The only person I care about who managed to get through it unharmed was my best friend, Eric. When I awoke in the hospital, I found him sitting at my bedside. It should have been comforting, but Eric was behaving strangely. He seemed worried about more than recent events, but wouldn't say what it was.

Then it got even weirder when my attorney, showed up with a Marine Colonel in tow. The

Colonel is in charge of some hush-hush military investigation involving Slotter, the renegade from special forces who shot Ginny.

They offered me a deal to avoid prosecution for two murders I didn't commit. One of the dead men was my boss, John Biggs, who was found hanging from the chandelier in his posh corner office after he got a call from a federal prosecutor.

I'm a lawyer, by the way. At least I was before the firm placed me on unpaid leave. A spendthrift spouse and strangling medical bills for my mother's long term health care have left me broke. So, I took a job working as a body guard for a monk named Padma Ganesha.

He wrote a bestselling book about the happiest place on Earth. Ginny somehow persuaded him to travel to Louisville and speak at a lecture series called, "Ideas to Change the World." It was held in an auditorium on Louisville's waterfront called, the Center. When I arrived, I found the security guard with a knife buried in his chest.

The evening went from bad to worse after Pony Tail started shooting. Thirty-two hundred peace loving hippies fought their way to the exits, only to find themselves locked inside. They are all dead now. According to the news reports, there was a gas leak, but I was told by the Marine

Colonel the gas leak is a cover story.

For some reason, the military wanted to cover up the truth and offered me immunity to keep quiet about what really happened. The deal was a huge insult to my intelligence. Even though I was in no mood to allow myself to be controlled by some military goon, I went along with it to get rid of them.

As soon as the Colonel left my room, I slipped out in the hopes of finding Slotter in the intensive care unit recovering from her own gunshot wounds. Following Slotter's arrest, a police detective stuck a pistol in her belly and pulled the trigger. The Jack Ruby moment was motivated by vengeance for the death of the detective's daughter at the Center.

Slotter had made a few enemies and we all wanted her dead, but it was beginning to look like she was under the protection of the same Colonel who was trying to hush up what really happened at the Center.

Instead of Slotter, I found Ginny alive and well in the intensive care unit. I thought for sure she was dead and now I was beginning to doubt my own memory of what happened. It was inconceivable that she took a bullet to the head and survived, let alone healed so quickly. At least it was inconceivable to a sane person.

I shook off the self-doubt. Something was

amiss, but if Ginny survived by some unknown miracle, then maybe, just maybe, Uncle Jim and Bird also survived. I could only hope, but for now I wanted to focus on what was right in front of me. Ginny was alive and that was huge.

Neither the nurse nor I knew what to say in response to the sight of her perfectly healed wound. It was Ginny who broke the silence.

"My father is still alive and I'm going to find him," said Ginny. "Will you help me, Grant?"

Ginny's father had disappeared years ago. For some reason, Slotter thought he was still alive and that's why she kidnapped Ginny. In some weird way, it must have given Ginny hope. I didn't think for a minute the man was still alive after all this time, but I wanted to be with Ginny and she wanted to search for him.

"Of course I will," I answered. "Where do you want to begin?"

"Brazil…he was last seen boarding a small plane for a tour of the Amazon Rainforest," answered Ginny without hesitation. "We'll begin there."

"That's a long time for someone to be missing," I said.

"I've never given up hope that my father is alive," she said. "One of the many reasons I opened a factory in Brazil was to pick up where the police left off with their investigation into his disappearance."

"What did they tell you?" I asked.

"Only that he charted a small plane and it never returned," she said.

"Where was it chartered?" I asked.

"Manaus, at the mouth of the Amazon," she answered.

"The Amazon Rainforest is huge," I said. "Do you know where he was headed?"

She shrugged.

"Nobody seems to know," said Ginny.

Something was bothering me about this story, but I couldn't quite put my finger on it. There were pieces of the puzzle missing and I had a nagging feeling I knew something about them.

"Do they know where the plane went down?" I asked.

"No," answered Ginny. "They spent a few days looking for the wreckage, but soon gave up when it couldn't be spotted from the air."

"Do you have plan?" I asked.

She nodded, but before she could answer, the nurse hit the emergency call button.

"You don't just walk out of ICU," barked Nurse Nightshade. "You're not going anywhere until Dr. Wiemp releases you."

Ginny stiffened. She looked like she was about to give the nurse a piece of her mind. I don't know about Ginny, but I don't like to be told what I can or can't do, especially by a stranger.

Still, no good ever comes from an unnecessary confrontation over something that is easily resolved. It was time for diplomacy, but before I could speak, Ginny snapped at the nurse.

"I'm not your prisoner," said Ginny.

Nurse Nightshade puffed her flat chest out as far as it would go.

"Rules are rules," she said. "You have to see the Doctor first."

"Not if she doesn't want to," I said. "As you can see, she's in perfect health."

The nurse shook her head.

"Who are you and what are you doing in my ICU outside of visiting hours?" she demanded.

Her attitude stunned me. It was time to kick it up a notch, so I extended my hand to her.

"My name is Grant Li, Attorney-at-Law," I said. "This woman does not need your permission to leave. Surely it's not your intention to hold her against her will."

Nurse Nightshade shrank from the extended hand, as if it held a poisonous snake. She opened her mouth to speak, but then abruptly shut it again. I think she was accustomed to patients following orders and our rebellion unbalanced her.

Between my martial arts training and law practice, I know a fighter when I see one. Nurse Nightshade was a fighter and wasn't about to lose a conflict with a couple of patients. She shifted her focus to the hospital gown I wore and somehow managed to regain her sense of power.

"You are a patient in this hospital and there is blood seeping from your bandages," said the nurse. "Let's get you back to your room before you hurt yourself."

I wasn't feeling my best and the bed rest she offered was tempting, but her tone annoyed me. I was about to say something I might regret when I heard footsteps outside of the door.

An arrogant voice barked a little too loudly, "This better be a real emergency."

A wave of relief passed over Nurse Nightshade's face. She could now pass the torch to someone else and that somebody happened to be wearing a name tag that identified him as, Jonathan Wiemp, M.D.

Dr. Wiemp was tall, but seemed much shorter thanks to a pronounced stoop. In addition to the stoop, he had a sag in the back of his neck that reminded me of a cartoon vulture I had seen one Saturday morning years ago.

In sharp contrast to an exceptionally pointed chin, he had a wide forehead with four rows of deep wrinkles spread across it. Thinning hair and grayish skin, gave him a haggard look.

It didn't get any better as you moved downward. A pot belly pushed the waist band of his slacks to the max. I didn't get a sense that the doctor took very good care of himself.

I guessed he was much younger than he appeared, but his clothes didn't help him look his age. They were old fashioned and added to his antique appearance. From the faded bow tie, to the heavily worn wing tip shoes, he looked like he had been wearing the same outfit since 1958.

Nurse Nightshade must have seen something different in Dr. Wiemp, because she never once took her doe eyed gaze from him. On the other hand, Dr. Wiemp hardly looked at her. My feelings about her softened considerably when I realized it would eventually end badly for her.

"This patient wants to leave, Doctor," said the nurse.

Dr. Wiemp scowled over the top of black rimmed glasses at Ginny. Leaving was not part of his prognosis. He expected her to be dead by morning. I saw something else in his face. This arrogant man disliked being wrong and found her recovery insulting.

"No one is leaving," said Dr. Wiemp in a raspy voice that told me he was a heavy smoker.

I had one of those random moments we all

have from time to time. For some odd reason, Dr. Wiemp's statement reminded me of the title to Jim Morrison's biography, "No One Here Gets Out Alive." The disturbing comparison was all I needed to abandon diplomacy and shift into full blown lawyer mode.

"Unless you step aside and allow her to leave, you will be prosecuted to the fullest extent of the law for false imprisonment," I said to Dr. Wiemp.

He looked me up and down before digging a hand into his pocket and pulling out a smartphone. He punched in a call and waited impatiently.

"We have a problem," he said into the phone. "Send security."

"Has everyone gone completely insane?" asked Ginny.

"This is ridiculous," I agreed. "We're leaving."

I took Ginny's hand and gently pulled her to her feet. At first, she submitted, but then looked down at her clothes. I followed her eyes. She was wearing one of those awful hospital gowns that invariably expose the patient's behind. In most instances, it's a behind I'd rather not look at, but as Ginny cut a path to the closet I enjoyed a lingering look at a backside that was flawless in a Barbie doll sort of way.

I had seen her in a bikini a few days earlier and hungered for more. I watched as she stuffed her things into a bag and grabbed my hand again.

As we headed to the door, I caught a glimpse of the nurse's hateful glare. She quickly cut her jealous eyes to Dr. Wiemp, who was standing in the door blocking our way. He didn't show any signs of yielding.

I looked straight into his eyes and with dead calm said, "You need to step aside, now."

Dr. Wiemp's arrogance seemed to dissipate. For the first time, he was unsure of himself. His eyes faltered and his gaze dropped to his feet as he stepped aside. I led Ginny into the hall where we ran smack into two huge security guards.

Dr. Wiemp's arrogance returned as he barked, "Take this man to the psychological services unit and put him in restraints."

Of all the things he could have said, Dr. Wiemp managed to say the only thing that could send me over the edge. Raw terror pushed me into berserker mode. In keeping with my training, I savagely attacked the biggest guard first, delivering multiple blows to his vital points within the first three seconds.

He was out cold and on his way to the ground when I disarmed the second security guard and pressed the 45 to his temple. I would have pulled the trigger too, but I heard something in Ginny's voice that pulled me from the brink.

"Oh, my God!" said Ginny. "Grant, no...please don't!"

Her voice saved the guard's life and it saved me from doing something that would have haunted me for the rest of my life. In the face of what might have been my hands started shaking uncontrollably. When I turned to Ginny, I was crushed by what I saw in her eyes. I wanted to explain and took a deep breath to gather myself, but felt something stab me in the neck and then I was out cold.

ABOUT ROBERT GRANT

Among Robert Grant's many interests are martial arts. He comes from a long line of Taoist, who left their sheltered lives in a mountain monastery to wander a world filled with raw beauty. These wandering monks have a long tradition of telling stories that both entertain and teach. Robert promised his sifu he would keep the tradition of storytelling alive and began developing a story idea that pitted a young lawyer/martial artist against a powerful pharmaceutical company in an epic conflict over a miracle cure. The hero wants to insure the cure is freely available to everyone, but powerful enemies want to suppress it. The result is a first rate thriller with a mystical twist that will have you laughing one minute and crying the next. Come, open a book and let your mind travel to places you never knew existed.

CONNECT WITH ROBERT GRANT

Thank you for reading *Naked Tao*. Drop me a note and share your thoughts on my book. Please tell your friends and family about my work. I am busy writing the next book. Lastly, I want to invite you to come and hang out with me.

Send your mail messages to:
Robert@NTPublishingCompany.com

Follow me on Twitter:
https://twitter.com/nakedtao

Like my Facebook page:
http://www.facebook.com/AuthorRobertWGrant

Follow me on Google Plus:
https://www.google.com/+RobertGrantNakedTao

Follow my blog at:
http://www.ntpublishingcompany.com

Welcome to our family and please remember to leave a review of Naked Tao.

Peace out,
Robert